PRAISE FOR *DEUS EX M*

"Hilarious and wrenching, *Deus Ex Machina* crashes the absurdities of our media culture with a pleasing *brio*, while never losing sight of the inhumanity bred in this new domain of unchallenged corporate hegemony, where everything is subordinate to the Show. And it never lets us forget that no one is immune from—and that everyone is accountable for—all of our toxic dreams of power."

—Jim Shepard,
author of *Project X* and *Like You'd Understand Anyway*

"A fabulous (in all senses of the word) novel, *Deus Ex Machina* manages simultaneously to be philosophical, absurd, kinda dirty, hilarious and, well, real—an idea the book itself deftly excavates. Think Shakespeare's *The Tempest* gone distressingly and wonderfully modern."

—Rivka Galchen,
author of *Atmospheric Disturbances*

"Searing, riveting, shockingly smart, and imbued on every page with a wicked sense of humor, *Deus Ex Machina* dissects the modern moment like nobody's business. Altschul fearlessly plunges into the heart of darkness—reality television—and finds the tragicomedy of our time there. Brave, bold, and moving work."

—Stacey D'Erasmo,
author of *The Sky Below*

"In his new novel, Andrew Foster Altschul has taken reality TV and turned it on its head, with characters that are sharp, funny, and ruthless. But if you look closer you'll see another story, about the nature of identity and the layering of selves that speaks volumes on the abstraction of media, and what it means to truly connect with one another."

—Hannah Tinti,
author of *The Good Thief*

"A sort of Gen X answer to Don DeLillo's boomer epic *Underworld*, it uses alt rock as a springboard to address all of the human condition." —*Minneapolis Star Tribune*

"A post-postmodern rock 'n' roll novel, entertaining and surprisingly elegant." —*Kirkus Reviews*

"A certain Seattle band is only the starting point of this smart, funny, breath-taking novel about celebrity, literature, and the elusive truth . . . *Lady Lazarus* is fun, sure, but Altschul is serious as a heart attack. This is a terrific book, big in scope, ambition and accomplishment." —*Uptown*

"Astounding . . . You've never read anything quite like it." —*San Francisco Magazine*

"Altschul is one of our great young writers, and *Lady Lazarus* is the proof. A poetic satire of rock and roll, and a rock and roll ode to poetry, it mirrors its heroine: smart, gorgeous, and funny as hell." —Andrew Sean Greer

"At last, a term for the self-destructive celebrities that so fascinate (and dominate) American culture: death artists . . . Andrew Foster Altschul covers a lot of ground here, and it's our entire culture— both high- and low-brow, pop and academic—that he rests his sights on." —*Sacramento News & Review*

"Some of the smartest, insightful, and flat-out funny writing about rock and roll celebrity since Neal Pollack's *Never Mind the Pollacks*." —*Blurt*

"Our fascinations with death and with fame have usurped our faith in art . . . but does anyone really care? Andrew Foster Altschul does. And so should we all." —*Solares Hill*

DEUS EX MACHINA

A Novel

∎

Andrew Foster Altschul

COUNTERPOINT · BERKELEY

This is a work of fiction. Names, characters, places, and incidents are the product
of the author's imagination or are used fictitiously. Any resemblance to actual
persons, living or dead, is entirely coincidental.

Library of Congress Cataloging-in-Publication Data is available.

978-1-58243-601-2

Cover design by Alvaro Villanueva
Interior Design by Neuwirth & Associates, Inc.

Printed in the United States of America

COUNTERPOINT
1919 Fifth Street
Berkeley, CA 94710

www.counterpointpress.com

Distributed by Publishers Group West

10 9 8 7 6 5 4 3 2 1

For V,

my favorite

"You have shown me a strange image, and they are strange prisoners."

"Like ourselves," I replied.

PLATO, *The Republic*

DEUS EX MACHINA

On the island they talk about everything, but they don't talk about love. Conversation is constant, even after the day's tasks are done, goals achieved, challenges met. Once they've banked the fire, posted a sentry, checked the stars one last time for messages, they collapse into a makeshift yurt, crawl beneath a ledge or igloo or shelter of hardened mud, huddle together for warmth—that's when the whispers arise: Did you hear something? Do you think they've forgotten us? I'm cold. How did this happen? Don't come near me. What in god's name is that smell?

Soon the dark is filled with talk of the day's ordeals, the uncertainty of tomorrow, the perfidy of strangers, a panoply of whims and yearnings no model can fully predict.

But never do they talk about love.

Occasionally one of the Deserted, troubled by a word or glance, leaves the shelter and wanders alone to speak of the unspeakable. We have excellent footage of these midnight soliloquies: a lone figure on the beach, or the tundra, a rising moon (for the moon is always rising), shadows of palm trees, suitable music, etc. In the past, the voice was sometimes garbled. A night breeze could ruin an entire sequence. Night breezes have been eliminated.

In daylight, a different story. The chatter is overwhelming—from the first rooster's crow (and today's roosters are real flesh-and-blood roosters) the Deserted peer out from hammocks, sleeping mats, bivvy sacks, pre-dug sand dugouts, squint into the high-res morning, and start talking: Another day in paradise. Sleep okay? Watch out for Leah, she's gunning for you. If I have to eat another squirrel. Those are my matches! She better watch out for *me*. Farouk looks pale. What the fuck am I doing here? Shut up and wash the gourds.

The producer hears every word. Every curse, every groan, every grumbled aside. Every stifled whimper, murmured comfort, every self-directed pep talk, every sigh. Every growl, every gasp. Every howl of terror and loneliness. He can listen in full-black, or play back a sequence on dozens of monitors. He can zoom in tight on a face or dolly out to a wider view. He can dissolve to a lofty bird's-eye. He can hold flat on one speaker, switch to shot/reverse; he can morph one face into another; he can cut to a flashback (or flashforward); he can drop in images of jungle or marine carnage. He has, at his disposal, over a dozen digital wipes. New software allows keyword searches, statistical analysis by phrase, speaker, group configuration, the results mapped against the island's grid, graphed for frequency, context, mood. At night, in private, he listens to everything at once, until the conversations of the Deserted blend into a fine white noise. He clears his mind, lets the deluge wash through him, listening for little treasures, like those that wash up on the island, from time to time, in precisely regulated intervals.

They talk of every conceivable topic, from auto repair to classic films to interest rates to existentialism, composting, zombies, dermatology, Swedish furniture. There are many discussions of menstruation and psychotherapy. Sports tend to fade off after Week Two. Food talk is never-ending and highly predictable; politics, rare. Every exchange, no matter how brief, is recorded, indexed, logged. At a secure site in Burbank, our vault holds terabytes of talk, archived for future study. The producer has remote access codes. In seasons past, he might stay awake for days, propped up by Red Bull and single-malt, listening to the Deserted's every word. He noted stolen glances, pregnant pauses, displaced aggression, private weeping, self-mutilation, painful confessions; he observed lingering touches, sudden alliances, clandestine sexual encounters of impressive variety. He waited. He waited. He paced his private quarters, tingling like a power cable, eventually collapsing in a frustrated sweat, filled with hatred for these people who never talk about love.

Now, he no longer cares. After twelve seasons he knows what to expect. He knows at a glance who will dominate and who will go forth aggrieved, who will succeed and who will betray, and who will quickly vanish from memory. He knows the palette of expression of which the Deserted are capable, its limited hues and textures. He eats well and sleeps on a strict schedule. His yoga teacher has shown him numerous relaxation techniques. He has given up alcohol entirely. He leaves the comprehensive playback review to his assistants.

But sometimes, at the end of the day, when the lighting takes a certain cast, he boots the monitor array in his private quarters, scans the island for a pleasant voice. He turns off his BlackBerry, dims the lights, floats in the cool blue glow of indicators and controls. Outside, the island is everywhere, a sea of darkness and disorder. But here, only the strained sounds of the Deserted come through. The software filters out interference, lets him focus on a pair of lips, the nape of a neck, the smooth back of a tanned hand. When he's found the voice he wants, casually chatting about cryogenics, he closes his eyes, slides down in his chair, and slowly masturbates.

WEEK ONE

■

Fade in. Dawn breaking over the dark face of the sea.

Daylight divides sky from ocean, to bring forth this uninhabited island, where ten unsuspecting people will spend the next seven weeks living, breathing, sleeping, and eating together, trying to stay alive. Their families, friends, and employers know nothing of their whereabouts. Hundreds of miles from civilization, there are no ATMs or cellphones, no day spas, no trips to the mall. Their real lives will become distant memories as they struggle to form alliances, guard against deception, and survive the island's dangers. No one can tell them where to go or what to do. Their fate is theirs, and only theirs, to determine.

They've come from all walks of life, but there's only one way off the island: a harrowing trek through some of the roughest terrain known to man. The Deserted have no maps, few supplies, only the clothes on their backs, their wits, their strength. Anything can happen. As they fight the elements and fight their fears, these ten competitors will have to learn to work together and forge a common purpose.

In the end, only one of them will make it to Paradise.

Who has the brains, the stamina, the ruthlessness to become Lord of the Island?

The weather is hot, the ocean churns. Watch: the flash of light in a tropical sky, the trail of dark smoke as a passenger jet goes down. Terrified screams in the cabin, vertiginous shivers of the handheld camera, the ominous cut to test pattern.

"Man, you see the jugs on that stewardess?" says an audio tech.

"They are called flight attendants," says the director.

"You see the flight attendants on that stewardess?"

"Shut up," says the producer.

Soon they appear: ten bobbing heads on the horizon, ten stunned and wounded figures clinging to suitcases and charred pieces of metal, kicking legs visible beneath the blood-clouded water. Below, a shark silently circles. As they drag their makeshift rafts up the narrow beach, collapse one by one in exhaustion and shock, the character generator puts up their information, written across the screen by a finger of fire:

Clarice Ochman, a systems analyst from El Paso, Texas.

Richard McMasters, a hairdresser from Long Beach, California.

Walter Bernatelli, a retired Marine sergeant from Virginia Beach.

Alejandra Ruiz, a high school math teacher from the Bronx.

Stan Clewes, an auto mechanic from Deston, Arkansas.

Hiroko Takamashi, a postal worker from Waukesha, Wisconsin.

Simon Willoughby, a poet from South Hadley, Massachusetts.

Candy Bright, a corporate lawyer from Denver, Colorado.

Shaneequio Jones, a gang outreach counselor from Watts, California.

And finally, leaning against a tree at the far edge of the crescent of sand: Gloria Hamm, a dental hygienist from Garden City, New York.

"Where's my coffee?" says the producer.

Take a good look as they tend their wounds, build their camp,

gather wood, scout the beach for useful items: a four-minute segment set to bouncy, vaguely African banjo music. Watch the
sidelong glances, the smiles of admiration. Listen to the halting
introductions, strategic compliments, innocent queries. Note the
determination in their eyes. The ex-Marine barks orders, squints at
the slow-moving poet. The math teacher scowls at the gang outreach counselor. The lawyer fixes her hair. Each figure backdropped
by the island's portentous landscape, the heavy forest looming over
them, stern gray mountains in the distance. The music fades. You
won't soon forget these ten. Already they're establishing their roles,
as though they've been preparing for this moment their entire lives.
They're a fine group: the resilient, the ambitious, the Deserted.

"Where in the name of Jesus H. Motherfucking Christ is my
coffee?" shouts the producer. The assistant producers ignore him.
The director purses his lips.

From the galley a terrified intern shouts, "Coming!"

At a forward console Miley, the junior AP, is texting the six field
team leaders. "Anything on the blogs?" the producer asks. "Just
give me the synopsis."

"Busy," says Miley, with a backward glance. The command center
teems with techs and interns, story assistants huddled against the
back wall, runners getting in everyone's way. The air is filled with
the tapping of keys, clicking of mice, orders barked into headsets, a
thunderous fart of unknown provenance. The producer keeps a cup
of rubber bands at his side, with which to reprimand anyone who
pauses in his line of sight.

"Belly ring on the blond, monitor five!" cries a logger.

"Holy shit, I think the math teacher's a double-D!" says another.

Taylette, the line producer on loan from Endemol, says, "Those
are so not real." An argument begins. The producer whistles, holds
up the cup of rubber bands, and they fall silent.

Shelters constructed, the Deserted turn to hunting and gathering, braving the edge of the rainforest, ten asynchronous images along the top row of the monitor wall. Alejandra and Clarice disappear in search of fruit while Shaneequio plunges into the sea with his switchblade. Richard and Hiroko start inventorying the flotsam luggage—they will find nothing of value, no articles of personal hygiene, clothes inappropriate for the island climate. They blink at the sun, draw forearms across brows. Bernatelli, his shirt off and tucked into his belt, shows Candy how to build a box fire, then stands behind her while she attempts her own, thrusting his pelvis and grinning at the others. Simon, the poet, nervously cleans a gash in his leg. All captured in a variety of cuts and dissolves from player to player, images racking in and out of focus, digital distortions and shifting saturations that foretell unpredictable events, ever-changing dynamics, relentless drama. It's all the video ops can do to maintain depth of field.

"Someone keeping an eye on G.I. Jane over there?" says Francisco, the senior AP, poached from Animal Planet in Season Four.

"More like Ranger Rick!" says Audio.

At the edge of the forest, Gloria Hamm squats on her haunches, honing a sharp, flat rock. She is thick-waisted, square-jawed. Wearing cargo pants and a faded burgundy T-shirt, she looks no different than if she were taking her car to the shop or cleaning her apartment. Her thin lips press tightly as she lashes the rock to a charred metal armrest.

"Didn't we decide no more dykes?" Francisco says. He goes by Paco, though his friends call him "El Lobo." "Wasn't there like a meeting on this?"

Patel, the director, says, "You believe what is said at a meeting?"

Two techs wrestle in front of the video toaster, sneakers squeaking on the rubber mats. One shoves the other aside in triumph, and on the line monitor appears a close-up of Candy's belly ring, the bleached scrim of hair disappearing below her waistline.

The victorious tech strokes the fade bar. "Bet you an eight ball that's not her only piercing."

"Not by the time I get done with her!" says the other.

The producer stretches a rubber band, scores a bull's-eye.

Shaneequio stumbles back to the beach, sans fish, and coughs up a thin string of vomit. Everyone in the command center cheers.

"Why does there always have to be a bimbo?" says Miley. She sits on the arm of the producer's chair. He tries not to play favorites, but ever since Miley's arrival in Season Six to clean up the Benin fiasco, the producer's job has been that much easier. "It's not even like they're that entertaining—anyone can see it's the math teacher who'll end up sucking cock in the woods."

"Anything from Burbank yet?" he asks. The irony being that Miley could pass for a bimbo herself—bleached blonde hair, sapphire contact lenses, the most spectacular tits money could buy. She's not shy about sticking them in your face, either. The only flaw in her appearance is a rough, raised scar that runs along her jaw and below her left ear, forking into her hairline. He's never asked her about it.

"Unless it's Richard," she says, nodding at the hand-wringing hairdresser. "Did you know it's pronounced *Ree-SHARD*? How do we get that on screen?"

"Burbank."

She looks down at him with practiced condescension. "It's four AM in Burbank. Boby hasn't even had his Cap'n Crunch yet." She peeks at her BlackBerry. "They'll make us sweat it a while. Try to enjoy yourself."

"Get off the chair."

"So we got us a dyke and a maricón, people," says Paco, addressing the back of the room. Story assistants tap vigorously on iPads. Paco is solid, broad-chested, his dark hair longish behind the ears. "Maybe there's a sub-arc in there? Someone's gotta storyline that shit." An alert goes off on his console. "Fuck me, you watching the poet, Bossman? His pulse is up to 130. Ask me, we got a panic attack coming."

"Camera Four, in on Simon," says Patel. "Audio, some breathing please?"

"Anything usable in his file?" Miley asks. "Meds? A therapist?"

"He's a poet, what do you think?" Paco says. "Boss, you checking this out?"

But the producer is not watching Simon, nor is he watching Clarice and Alejandra burying a private stash of tangerines, nor Candy giving Bernatelli a shoulder rub. His eyes are on Gloria Hamm, the dental hygienist. Using her homemade hatchet, she has amassed a small woodpile. Her upper arms are as thick as Paco's, her hands callused and meaty on the metal shaft. She's spoken to no one, ogled no one, stayed out of everyone's way. Big-boned, olive-skinned, her face plain and vaguely bored. Her short hair does not blow attractively in the wind. She does not wear sunglasses, cutoff jeans, or a sarong; she does not have sculpted abs or any visible tattoos. Put bluntly, she's nondescript, a dud—just the kind of thing they can't afford. Not this season.

"How the hell did she get here?" he says.

"We're all in this together, and I want you to know I'll be looking out for every one of you," says Bernatelli, standing before the group, hands on hips. "Like in the song—you can lean on me, when you're not strong." They're all around the fire, backlit by an enhanced dusk, shucking mussels with sandy fingers. A small rodent roasts on a spit. Still shirtless, Bernatelli points to a tattoo on his biceps. "We have a saying in the Marines: *Semper fi.* Always loyal. That's Walter Bernatelli."

With a groan, Gloria Hamm turns and stalks back to the tree line. Bernatelli folds his arms and watches her drag a long tree limb onto the sand and start kicking it to bits, throwing the pieces on the woodpile.

"Uh oh," says the chyron master. "Dyke versus Marine!"

"Don't make me angry," says Audio. "You wouldn't like me when I'm angry!"

"The next person who talks gets my foot up their ass," says the producer. "Plus, you're on the next canoe back to Indonesia. Now shut the fuck up."

A silence of stifled laughter fills the command center. Miley, still on the chair, regards him with raised, perfectly plucked eyebrows.

Bernatelli assigns cleanup chores, then drifts toward Gloria and leans casually against a tree. "Want me to take over?" She says nothing. "Relax. Let someone else do some work," he says. In the gentle light of stars and ocean, his torso looks cast in granite, sand adhering to his hard, hairless pecs.

Gloria plants her feet, leans back, and snaps a four-foot branch.

"Don't want to burn out." Bernatelli taps the side of his head, lowers his voice. "Strong players like you and me gotta always be thinking. Gotta delegate."

"Touch her!" says the chyron master. "Grab her ass!" says a logger.

"Ready cross-two, Camera Three," says Patel, and on the preview monitor the angle changes so the back of Bernatelli's head partially eclipses Gloria's face. On another screen the next shot is lined up: two tiny figures backdropped by the encroaching rainforest, the falling night. "Is she going to answer him?" Patel turns to Paco, who shrugs. "Suzy," he says into his headset, "can't you get her to say something?"

Gloria turns away. Behind her back, Bernatelli gives her the finger.

Shot of the camp, the other Deserted bedding down in the shelter. Simon, shivering, cleans his wound again. Shaneequio, lying on his back like a mummy, swats angrily at a cloud of sandflies. Someone hums a lullaby; someone says, "Goodnight, John-boy."

"And . . . *bottle*," Patel says. At the edge of the beach, a blackened bottle buoys up from the sea, teases and spins lazily on the waterline. Faintly, the strained chords of the theme music—reinterpreted this season as a pop-punk anthem—fade in. Miley confirms overnight rotation with the field teams. Paco runs diagnostics, assigns video and audio backup. Patel calls in camera specs for the morning's ordeals.

The producer watches them a moment longer: the Deserted, this group of ten strangers who, by instinct alone, are already falling into familiar, dramatically useful dynamics. All except Gloria Hamm. Market research would suggest she's a nonstarter, that she'll be gone by Week Three. Quietly, while the APs are busy, the line producer harassing the techs, he leans over his laptop, brings a spycam in tight on her face. She blinks at the moon, expressionless; she seems barely aware of the others. What had casting seen in her? Out of thousands of auditioners, why choose this one?

Soon enough Gloria turns on her side and falls asleep. All around the command center, people are logging out of terminals, signing off on clipboards, making plans for late-night poker. The sound techs have started their pool, claiming dibs on whom they plan to fuck in the off-season. Interns stand at the perimeter, staring at their feet and furiously IMing each other.

Far from the Facility, far across the island's desolate expanses, its lush rainforest and parched salt flats, its raging rapids and wheat-dry savanna and treacherous thickets of quicksand, beyond the Ancient Ruins and the Mangrove Swamp and the Unnavigable Canyon and the seething Cobra Pit, the badlands surge toward stony peaks, a stern mountain range that lops off the northern expanse of old-growth forest and placid, sparkling Paradise Beach.

The producer's yoga teacher insists he seek solitude: no APs, no dailies, no spreadsheets, no GPS. No toadying editors or ambitious interns gibbering at his ankles like puppies in a pet store, no phone calls from tabloid writers who've blown someone in Burbank for the number. The wind and the sun, the silence of the skies and the silence of his thoughts—he needs these things now, more than he needs single-malt scotch and young pussy.

He stands atop a broad escarpment, most of the island laid out before him. Squinting, he can just make out the cranes and backhoes busying through the Ancient Ruins, six miles distant, the sun stabbing off the steel and glass of the Facility to the southwest. He can see the cut in the eastern forest where trucks roll through from Beachhead A and a dim glow near the island's center he assumes is the Volcanic Labyrinth. But he cannot see the Deserted, not even a plume of smoke from their campfire. It's an enormous relief, like taking off clothing that fits too tight. But it's also deeply unsettling, as though he's somehow misplaced a vital organ.

"Prove it," Armand had said over the phone, the night before. "Show them the well's not dry. Remember what you've accomplished." Fourteen years ago Armand discovered the producer hosting a cable home-improvement show and gave him his shot. Now Armand lives in San Miguel de Allende, forced into retirement by the recent coup in Programming, replaced by a twenty-eight year old MBA transferred from Finance.

"What we've accomplished. And remind me what that is?"

"Self-pity doesn't suit you." Armand sighed. "Maybe you're right. Maybe it's time for a rest. The inmates are running the asylum. Old soldiers like us have seen our day." But that's not quite right, the producer thought. The inmates are running the *whole world*—only they're turning it into the asylum. In the end, they seemed to prefer the asylum. "Tennyson," Armand said. "What was it? *A last noble challenge for men who once strove with gods . . .*"

"Ulysses never strove with Boby al-Hajj," the producer said, referring to the new senior VP for programming.

"True, true."

Fourteen years ago, Armand showed up on location at *The Wrecking Ball* with an entourage of clean-cut young men in hand-tailored suits; the producer's first thought had been that he was being audited. After two months of meetings, mostly held at the wet bar on the roof of Armand's Brentwood home, they were ready to go to the network. Two years later, the producer had his first Emmy.

"You remember Season One?" he said. "How terrified we were all the time?"

"Well, really—the fashion sense of those people," Armand said. "I refuse to set foot in Florida ever again."

"We had no idea what they would say. What they might do. It was a seven-week high-wire act," the producer said, glancing at the first cut of the beach arrival. Shots of Candy, the lawyer, stuffing her bra; of Richard, the hairdresser, voguing with Clarice while Shane-equio beat-boxed from the blackened frame of an airplane seat; of Simon, the poet, trying to scribble something on bark. "Feels like a long time ago," he said.

"At the time you weren't so pleased," Armand said. "Unless all that Xanax was a measure of your joy."

"It's just so predictable now. Every word, every scheme. Whatever happened to free will?"

"Free will wreaks havoc with underwriting, as you well know."

The producer sighed. On the screen, Bernatelli did one-arm pushups in the sand while Stan, the mechanic, shoved a plug of tobacco behind his lower lip. Alejandra combed her long, shiny hair, staring dreamily toward the horizon, and the producer was startled by a memory of his wife, standing at her easel, her eyes moving past him as though he weren't there. He closed his eyes and reached for the small stone he keeps in his pocket, squeezing it until the image receded.

"Maybe Boby's right," he said then. "Maybe reality's a younger man's game."

"It's a comfort, that's all." Through the phone he heard Armand take a long drag from a cigarette. "People like to find themselves on television. That's all they really want. Don't get philosophical. If it's the last time, have fun with it. Relax. Make it your monument."

But if it's a monument, he thinks, so far it's a monument to every other season, a closed loop. At least on *The Wrecking Ball* they'd built things, however ugly and extravagant; they'd had something to show for the effort. What did they have here, except for obsessive fan clubs, a bestselling line of Season Ten action figures, and four hundred and eighty-five thousand Facebook friends?

"You like it down there?" he'd said to Armand. In the background he heard a voice calling in Spanish.

"Oh, you know . . . pretty houses, pretty boys. The doors here are exquisite. They're famous, you know, hand-carved, beautiful scrollwork. You can spend a whole afternoon just walking down the street. Frankly, the place looks a bit like Disneyland. Sí, sí, I'm coming," he called to someone. "I'm trying to get Liz down for a visit."

"How is she?" Armand's daughter had worked at the Burbank office for a while, until the suits grew impatient with her vodka-and-pills habit and nudged her onto disability. Last he'd heard, she was in rehab, having progressed to cocaine and driven a rented Hummer through her ex-boyfriend's ex-wife's living room wall.

"She's learning macramé," Armand said, a smile in his voice. "I think we should all learn macramé. I must go to breakfast now," he'd said. The producer had thought it was nighttime in Mexico. "Señora Carmen gets annoyed when I'm late."

Now, from his stony vantage, the producer watches a cargo ship a mile off the island's eastern shore. Gun-metal gray, network logo emblazoned on the prow, the ship cleaves a silent wake through the sea's corrugated glimmer. Design got underway eighteen months ago; of thirty-four major construction jobs, only the Ancient Ruins are unfinished, plus a few last patches to the microwave relay grid. What labors, what small miracles of coordination, to create this untouched island. Our people span continents, fill warehouses, ride cubicles, carry all manner of handheld scanning devices; invisible frequencies throb with instructions from Shanghai to São Paulo; queries fly sharp as chatter in a monkey house. The Deserted know none of this. They see no evidence of human intervention. They'll be kept to the island's southeast corner, far from the beachhead and the Facility, until the ruins are complete, snakepits populated, footprints erased from the island's every pristine inch.

Breathing heavily, pulse pounding, he stops on a wide stretch of trail, high above the tree line, and lets the island's smells fill his skull. Broken rock, eucalyptus, the distant tang of the ocean: the high wind gives these things a sharpness that makes his fingertips tingle. The light chill, the sting of sun on his scalp—these cannot be fabricated. He stretches his arms over his head, sucks in air, thinks, not for the first time: Why not a show about people enjoying a beautiful day?

Then laughs to himself, imagining Boby's face.

The trail narrows along the edge of a high wall of rock, a drop of several hundred feet down to the forest. Fifty yards higher, an ancient rockslide fills a wide bowl in the mountainside. Splintered wood spars and lengths of rusted sheet metal jut from the scree. The network's holding company had acquired the island from a bankrupt mining outfit. It had taken three years to make the place hospitable enough to bring a crew, and still they are forbidden, at the underwriters' insistence, to eat anything that grows or grazes in the island's soil. A clause in each player's contract indemnifies the network against "food-related medical liability."

In the distance, the network ship has dropped anchor off the beachhead, a litter of launches racing out across the water like piglets to the teat. Needing to take a piss, the producer scrambles over loose rocks and spots a narrow opening in the mountainside, partially blocked by small boulders. The network maps said nothing about a cave. Most of this sector was shaded out, marked BALLARD CORP. OPERATIONS ZONE. HR would have a fit if they knew he were here. He peers back along the trail, out toward the gleaming Facility. "Like a sinking star!" he cries—Tennyson again—scoffs at his own theatrics and squeezes past the boulders.

The cave smells of ammonia and rotting meat, an acrid tang of metal that scrapes in the back of his throat. He pulls his shirt collar over his mouth and nose and shuffles in a few yards, gloom slipping over him like a bank robber's mask. Feeling for a wall with his free hand, he waters the stone with piss and squints farther into the dark. The floor is slick with an oily slime; after a dozen yards he can feel the roof lowering. He has no flashlight, not even a cigarette lighter. In his pocket, one hand feels for the small stone, turns it over and over, smooth and cool against his fingertips.

The space opens up again, cold and disembodying; he has the feeling of floating unmoored, his sense of direction faltering. He turns back to look for the opening, a thin gray rift in the black distance. Sound is strangely distorted, as though different mixes are coming through different channels; he can't tell if the scuffling in his ears is the echo of his footsteps or the defensive movements of something feral and blind. He slides his feet, imagining a deep chasm with every step, but keeps going, heart quieting, breath slowing into keen concentration. Mindfulness. There's something here, something strange and numinous, something he ought to be able to use—but he doesn't want to think too hard about it yet. Better to let it germinate, worm its own slow route into his consciousness. This is where twelve seasons' ideas have come from:

glimmers nursed with days of silence, unresponsive to everyone around him. Armand used to joke that it was a "quasi-autistic" kind of genius. His wife called it "going away," as in: Why bother coming home?

When something slaps against the side of his head he cries out and crouches, one palm squelching in guano. The air is troubled and thick over his head, the sound of his breathing almost deafening, broken up by a rush of flutters and squeals as the cave mouth fills with quotation marks that bunch together and blow apart and disappear.

Bats!

There were bats in Benin, too. Bats in the Tetons. Paco wanted to work bats into Antarctica, but it tested badly. Penguins were all the rage that season, thanks to that documentary. Still, it's been a while, he thinks, carefully straightening, slowing his breath the way his yoga teacher showed him. They ought to be able to do something here on the island. The sprout of an idea inches a little higher as he makes his way back to the entrance.

Eyes adjusted, he stops just before the opening to frame a shot through the crooked gash: treetops, ocean, a sliver of the command center's curved metal roof. Nothing that can't be doctored out. He examines what at first look like brown smudges on the rock wall, but upon closer inspection turn out to be drawings, climbing up and around the entrance, arranged in haphazard rows. He runs his fingertips over the crude images, feels the texture of these shallow etchings in the rough stone: stick figures, arrows, a sun and a moon, something that's either a giant spider or a bear. Higher up, a tableau of a violent ocean, towering waves; something that looks like a mountain breaking in two, a hunting party attacking it from above and below. A bird.

The producer frowns at the drawings. What were they trying to say? All this time in their shit-stinking cave, and all they drew was what they saw every day. Why couldn't he find a symphony written in the stone? The Special Theory of Relativity? Some unimagined wisdom of the ancients? But no, it turns out the island's long-ago inhabitants were just as banal as the Deserted. His three-year-old niece could have drawn this crap.

Five, he corrects himself. His niece is five. Or six.

Still, he stares at the drawings for a long time, squeezing the stone in his pocket. His pulse slows; his vision narrows against the backdrop glare. Something, he thinks. There's something here, something more than local flavor. We've got more local flavor than we know what to do with. We've got binders full of it, wardrobe assistants paid to think of nothing else. But this is different.

Beyond the cave mouth the wind is rising. The gusts resolve into the sound of rotors, a pall of grit blowing across the stone, the whine and roar of the network helicopter rising out of the basin. Time to get back to work. He looks for a stick to scrape the drying shit off his shoes but decides not to bother.

Back at the command center, all the clocks are blinking and everyone is wearing green visors.

"She punked his ass, Bossman!" says Paco, trying to distract the producer from the fact that the AP is in his chair. "Bluffed his shit on kings and fours, while that fuckin redneck's sitting on a full house."

On the big screen, Candy, the corporate lawyer, sweeps a pile of shells across a felt-covered table. The rest of the Deserted shake their heads and glower, slap mosquitoes off their necks, sweating it out in the broken light of the Poker Pavilion.

"Good rack beats a good brain every time," says the chyron master.

"She clouded his mind and shit!" cries Camera Five, zooming on Candy's makeshift halter top.

"'The Gambler'? How old is this song?" says the producer. "Which creative genius came up with that? And what's with the clocks?"

Stan Clewes, the mechanic, sits very still, watching Candy count her shells. Her top does seem suspiciously tight. "What's a fellow got to do to win his money back?" he says, just the right hint of nastiness in his voice. Then he spits a gout of tobacco juice into a half-coconut.

"Make me an offer," she says.

"Out of the chair, Paco," says the producer.

A kid from Facilities drags a stepladder below the digital monitor clock, which is now speeding endlessly through its numbers. "Fuck out of the way!" says the chyron master. The remote camera operators are up in arms. A barrage of crumpled paper and banana peels flies across the monitors. The kid from Facilities beats a retreat.

"How about let's raise the stakes. Winner sleeps in, everyone else has firewood duty at dawn?" Bernatelli, the ex-Marine, shuffles cards at the head of the table. He's done a masterful job installing himself as de facto leader, setting himself up nicely for a mid-season Oedipal revolt, or possibly a reformed-sinner sympathy grab. Maybe both. Either way, the producer hopes he gets his teeth knocked out before it's all over. "Or shall we say boys against girls, back rubs for the winners?" He winks at Stan; Simon, the poet, and Alejandra, the math teacher, roll their eyes. Richard, the hairdresser, nods off in his seat, drool gleaming on his chin.

"How about let's raise the stakes," someone in the back of the control room says. "How about I pork you with my bayonet?"

"Looks like someone already porked Ree-*shard* in the mouth," says Audio, to an eruption of snickers.

"'Pork'?" says Taylette. "Who the fuck says 'pork'?"

The message in the bottle had led them half a mile into the interior, promising "the islands trezhur to them with luck and nerve."

Scanning the ISO monitors, the producer doesn't see much nerve, but he does see ten unshowered, pissed-off people slouched in cane chairs like high school students in detention. Hiroko flails desperately at the flying beetles that zoom through the light. Clarice, the systems analyst, can't stop scratching her groin. But when a camera goes hot, suddenly they're all attention, a picture of focus and determination, the killer instinct glinting in their eyes. They're professionals, this group, not to be underestimated. All except Gloria Hamm, pale and a bit pouchy of cheek and neck. She squints at the others as though they are speaking a foreign language, looks around the pavilion like a tourist lost in a bus station.

"How was the hike? You find your chi out there or what?" Miley stands at the producer's side, scribbling on a clipboard.

The producer checks his BlackBerry: nothing from Boby. He's not sure if that's a disappointment or a relief. "What do you hear from the ruins?"

"We're good," she says. She's still scribbling, her grip on the pen turning her fingers white. "Tomorrow or the next day. Time to spare."

"They'll have the sundial working?"

She sits on the edge of the chair, gets up again. She's barefoot, wearing tight, camo-colored capris, a peach tank top with the network logo unfurling across the tits. In Benin she'd been a godsend, the rest of the crew too traumatized to function. She took over all communication with the field teams, who had been frantic after losing contact with the Facility. She liaised with the State Department and private security companies, arranged an overnight shipment of Demerol for the producer and a surprise visit by his yoga teacher. She was the only person on the crew who spoke French, and she spoke it flawlessly. She even organized an impromptu game of laser tag, surprising in its fury, a necessary catharsis for those who remained at the Facility. In the off-season the producer visited her at her condo in Manhattan Beach with a two-thousand-dollar bottle of Burgundy and the keys to a rented villa near Cabo. They'd drunk the bottle on her balcony, but when it was time to leave for the airport she kissed him on the cheek, squeezed his balls, and said, "No offense, but you couldn't keep up."

"Looking ahead, some problems with the Volcanic Labyrinth," she says. "Tricky angles. Melting lenses. Hector says the remote cams won't last three weeks; we might have to do it all with field teams."

"So we'll do it all with field teams."

"Might want to check with the union on that one."

"Get Paco on it."

She sits by his arm again, gets up again, knocking the cup of rubber bands into his lap. "Oh, shit. Sorry! Too much coffee."

"Try cutting that coffee with some aspirin," he says. On the line monitor, an overhead of the poker table, ten heads bent over the green felt. "Give me a fucking break with this shot," he says. "What is this, ESPN? Someone give me some real television."

"Camera Four," says Patel. From his station in front of the monitors, Camera Four says, "At your service!" The other cameras tell him to shut up.

In the pavilion, Simon, the poet, is cleaning up, to the annoyance of Bernatelli and Candy. "*Suckaz,*" he says sardonically, as though making fun of himself and how unconvincing his trash talk must sound. The wound on his leg is not healing well, tropical bacteria breaking down cell walls, infiltrating his lymphatic system— though all the poet knows is it itches like hell. Shaneequio, his left eye bright with a crimson slick, counts his shells, then counts them again. Candy pushes back from the table, walks off to squat in the woods. When the next hand is dealt, Gloria Hamm tosses her cards on the felt.

"What would you think about a cave?" the producer asks Miley.

"I don't know. Sure. What cave? Run it by Boby. Wait, no, don't. Let that sleeping dog whatever, right?" She pounces at her laptop computer. "For Christ's sake, it's getting cloudy. How are they going to see the stars if it's cloudy?"

From across the room Paco says, "What the fuck, cloudy? Supposed to be clear for days." A heavy fog is oozing in from the south, congealed soup spilled on a glass table. "Man I told you not to hire him. Kid don't know shit about the weather."

"That is not fair," says Patel. The new weather engineer is his wife's cousin, brought in from Hyderabad at the last minute. "You can't blame one person for a team failure."

"Just saying, cabrón, your boy ain't ready."

"Calm the fuck down, people," the producer says. "If we don't get it tonight, we'll get it tomorrow."

"But—" Miley stops when she sees the producer's face. "Okay. Right."

"I don't know, Bossman," Paco says, feigning deep concern. "The rundown says tonight. You talking about messing with chronology? Don't seem like you."

"Leave me alone, Paco," he says.

Simon wins another hand, laying down three kings and provoking groans from Shaneequio and Stan. Bernatelli chews his lower lip. Alejandra, hair cascading over one shoulder, elbows the poet and says, "Sore losers."

"I ain't sore yet," Stan says to the math teacher. "Maybe an hour from now, if you're lucky."

Simon, raking his shells, tries to contain his elation. It's the one and only time he'll look like a winner, doomed by his slight build and careful speech. He's a poet, after all. He lives the life of the mind. He embodies neither ruggedness nor ruthlessness nor unrelenting faith. His extraction has been planned since before he laid eyes on the island. Any other fate would seem overdetermined. The sponsors would not like it at all.

"There once was a dude from South Hadley," says the chyron

master. He turns to the room, waiting for someone to pick it up. Story assistants scratch their heads. Camera One grabs a pencil.

Finally an intern offers, "He wanted to bang the math teacher so badly?" The intern gets a round of applause. A few green visors twirl into the air.

"Yo, Bossman, check it out," says Paco. "Bernatelli needs one card for a flush."

"So?"

Paco crosses his arms. "You're gonna let this little weasel walk off with the pot?"

"That's right."

"Puta madre, he's worse than that software developer we had in Mongolia. A ten of clubs—"

"Not how the show works," the producer says, checking the BlackBerry again. Still nothing from Boby. The poker match had, of course, been Boby's idea; only a phone call from Miley had convinced him that Playboy bunny dealers might strain what was left of credibility. "We don't intervene," he says.

"What about the weather? You just said—"

"That's editing. It's different."

Paco shoots Miley a look. "I'm just saying, Bossman, one little card—"

"I don't care what you're saying. How about you log the clips of them building the shelter like I asked you? I want a decision list by tomorrow, for next week's lead-in. And find some real music." Out of the corner of his eye he sees Miley gesturing for Paco to stay calm. Cameras Two and Three are having a slap fight. The clocks have stopped blinking and gone dark. The producer lowers his voice. "It's one thing to shape what already happened, Paco. Changing it is something else."

Paco rubs his chin. "Doesn't seem so different to me."

"Let's just wait and see, okay?" Animal Planet had countered by offering Paco a show in which players shared confined spaces with poisonous animals. Paco took forever to decide. Armand had led him to believe the producer was headed for a "Created By" role within a few years. Then Benin.

"Your funeral, B," Paco says, snatching up a clipboard and heading for the door. "Sure Boby's gonna dig some pussy poet closing the episode. Ought to help us a lot."

Audio techs shake their heads. Interns clear a path. Taylette says, "Lobo . . ."

"Let him cool down," says Miley, crouched by the director's chair.

"Oh, boy!" says Patel, half rising from his seat. On the big screen, Stan and Shaneequio are getting into it, the mechanic spitting on the dirt floor of the pavilion, the gang counselor reaching for his switchblade. Bernatelli and Clarice try to pull them apart. Around the control room, shouts egg them on. Audio hands Taylette a ten-dollar bill. Pan shot of the other players sitting at the table with stunned, nervous expressions.

"He just wants what's good for the show," Miley says, her voice close enough to startle the producer. "There's a lot riding on this season."

"If it's not the show, it's not the show."

"The show's whatever you say it is," she says. "You're the boss."

He looks at his junior AP, whose eyes are clear, too bright. His battle axe, he's often thought, his fixer. But who knows now, with the network second-guessing every scene, Boby climbing up everyone's ass. She's got a career to think about—they all do. It's not just the rats who abandon a sinking ship.

"Sometimes I wonder," the producer says.

The Deserted are back at the table, Simon's grin half hidden behind his winnings. On top of the pile of shells are Bernatelli's sneakers and a gold cross on a chain. "One more hand, everyone all in?" says the ex-Marine. One by one the players shove their chips into the pot. Simon eyes Bernatelli nervously. Audio switches to dynamic mics and suddenly the studio is flooded with the cold melody of cicadas. A distant owl hoots portentously, then hoots twice more, until the producer shoots Audio a look.

"Why not?" the poet says. He can barely contain his excitement. "All in!"

The producer stays to watch the deal, to peek over Gloria Hamm's shoulder: she's got a five, a nine, and a queen, two-suited, nothing to help her in the flop. For a split second, he considers changing that five to a king. But then he logs out, nods to Miley, and heads for the door, deepening his breathing to prepare for meditation. When he steps outside the command center, he can hear the ocean, off-duty crew members calling to each other in the dark, but not a whisper of cicadas.

Turning back, he catches a glimpse of Miley saying something in Patel's ear. The director nods, calls something to the cameramen. Runners move to and fro, silent shadows hustling before dozens of flickering screens. The main clock now reads 12:00.

There was something in that cave, something calm, immune to anything they are doing here. He thinks again of the unsettling emptiness, the crude drawings from a million years ago. There was something sacred about those drawings. Sacred and utterly futile.

As the door eases shut, he hears Simon's voice, heavy with convincing disappointment: "Fold."

WEEK TWO

■

. . . previously

They came to a desolate place, ten strangers stranded by accident, destined by cruel fate to wrest control of this barren, inhospitable island. Food, clothing, shelter—everything was lost in the crash. No one could tell them how to get home. They set out to tame their environment, to provide for themselves and for each other. They found fruits and nuts in the forest, fish and mussels in the sea. Stan took charge of chopping wood, while Bernatelli made a fire and led the others in building a shelter. By the end of Week One, things were looking up. But tensions are growing. Not everyone accepts Bernatelli's leadership. The other women are jealous of Candy's closeness with the ex-Marine. Shaneequio's temper is starting to flare. Hiroko has a secret stash of airline pretzels. Simon proved his prowess at the Poker Challenge, but his wounded leg is septic and growing critical. As they enter their second week, the players are battling hunger and homesickness, fighting to keep up their strength, outsmart their companions, and find their purpose. It's a tall order, full of desperate challenges and perilous choices. But the sun is shining, and hope springs eternal, and nothing is impossible for the ten valiant Deserted . . .

He's got a five-bedroom at the top of Laurel Canyon, a condo in Mumbai, and a 10 percent share in a tiny key east of St. Barts. He's got a mint 1958 Corvette and a limited-edition Bentley, closets full of hand-stitched Italian suits, a home entertainment system that's triggered lawsuits. He's got private jets at his disposal and a wine cellar recently featured in *GQ*. But the producer's prized possessions are rocks.

He's collected them from every corner of the world: deserts, prairies, barrier reefs, pre-Columbian ruins, Pleistocene formations, catacombs, ice floes. Varied in size, shape, and color, veined with metal or jutting with jagged crystal, his collection is housed in a teak showcase that goes, by contract, wherever he goes, sitting like a monument in his private quarters.

The quarters themselves are spartan, a double-wide trailer with raised ceilings and hardwood floors, half of which is taken up by his meditation space. No one may enter without invitation; by standing order the APs may call the red phone only in case of nuclear war or act of God. Back in the day, he'd wait until Week Seven and then bring some twenty-year-old intern here, fuck her acrobatically on the hardwood while rain-scented mist shot from atomizers in the walls and hidden speakers played Tibetan chants recorded by his yoga teacher. But no longer. This season he spends his off-hours in the lotus position, sipping green tea and contemplating rocks.

The one he keeps in his pocket is the newest addition to the collection, a reddish ovoid no bigger than a dog tag, cracked obliquely and speckled with shiny black chips. He found it one morning last spring on the northern edge of Puget Sound. He was sprinting barefoot on a secluded, stony beach—the soles of his feet shredding, a blinding ecstasy of pain that shot up into his jaw and forced a high howl into his throat; bleeding and exhausted, he stopped, needing something hard in his hand, needing to throw it with enough force to dislocate his shoulder. Arm cocked, he caught sight of an airplane, a glint at low altitude banking toward distant Seattle, and stopped.

The plane, silent and tiny, glided down through the sky. "No more," he'd said, panting a cold cloud. He slowed his breathing, knelt on the beach, let the pain diffuse through his body. This rock would mark the end of it, he decided, a symbol of his decision to leave the pain behind. He squeezed it until his hand throbbed, then slipped it in his pocket and limped back into the woods.

Later, in his tent, he would think about that airplane, how small and fragile it was, tilting on one wing, sliding silently back to the world. It was like the stone—heavy and solid, just as likely to fall out of the sky and disappear in the dark water. All the people on board would be lost. It could not be predicted or edited: It would just happen. Five weeks earlier they'd found his wife's car at the bottom of a ravine, off a service road in the Angeles National Forest. The car had burned, killing her and the man she'd left him for. Their bodies—bones and muscle and hair and nails—were fused into the upholstery and springs. They'd had to identify them by their teeth.

In his private quarters, the producer powers the monitors on the bedroom wall, logs into the system, and punches up the first cuts of yesterday's crossbow hunt, a near-catastrophe that has already elicited a volley of stern emails from Legal. Still no word from Boby. Paco and Miley wave off his growing concern, but the producer thinks he knows what's happening: the new VP, this twenty-something hair-gel addict in alligator shoes, this absinthe-sipping, Twitter-loving Wharton-grad thumbsucker, is sweating him. And he's right.

"La plus ça change," Armand had said. "Remember when we were the young Turks?"

"I remember when you were a young Greek. Come to think of it, I remember when you were an old Greek."

Over the phone, Armand sighed. "Wasn't that fun? Now I'm just another saggy gringo. But at least I have a tan. And my *español* is getting *mejor*."

"Terrific," the producer said. "Next season, Mexico?"

"The Deserted?" He heard Armand light a cigarette and wearily blow out the smoke. "I don't think so. They couldn't stand the isolation."

Now, in his inbox, there's a photo from Armand of the sidewalk cafés of Guanajuato. The caption reads, "It's not Paris, but then again I'm not Jean-Paul Belmondo." There are a dozen messages on the listserv about the Volcanic Labyrinth, an email from the dining complex reminding the crew to bus their trays, a link from Patel to some website about uranium. Starting Season Eleven, he'd let it be known that his quarters would thenceforth be offline, to cut down on distractions from his meditation. That had lasted less than two weeks, but the pretense has been useful to maintain.

For half an hour he runs searches in the database—conversations about caves, bats, poetry, corporate lawyers, dentistry. Season Two: The Deserted shelter for a night in a cave in the Maghreb. Season Eight: The Deserted, blindfolded, search a cave in the Grand Tetons for new iPod Shuffles. Season Ten, a college baseball coach named Steve LeBlanc says: "I wish I could crawl into a cave some-where and die." Also Season Ten, a lawyer gives a cop a hand job in a freshly dug trench. "Caveat emptor," says an insurance adjustor, Season Eleven, after cheating a pediatrician out of dinner. There have been five previous lawyers, one dentist, one periodontist, a grantwriter who once published a chapbook of poetry. Results related to bats take up four screens. Our newest software records the producer's search terms, runs them through statistical analyses, cross-references them with recent performance evaluations, Nielsen ratings, quarterly assessments written by his therapist. A report is being generated as we speak.

On the monitors, Stan Clewes is scrubbing bamboo plates in a barrel. "All's I'm saying is, we don't need 'em both. Just dead weight is all," he says to Bernatelli. Both wear makeshift aprons, Bernatelli shirtless once again. "One little faggotty dude is enough, right?"

Bernatelli's posture doesn't change, the muscles in his back and shoulders dancing as he works. His neck blisters with sunburn. "You're just pissed cause he took your money again."

"Took yours, too, Sarge," says Stan, then fires a shot of tobacco spit over the barrel. Bernatelli looks at him hard. "It don't matter about the money. I'm just saying when shit gets tough, who do we want around?"

"What about Shaneequio?"

"What about him?"

The ex-Marine shrugs. Cut to Alejandra, Hiroko, and Richard, strolling down the beach; Simon changing the dressing on his wounded leg; Shaneequio sitting on a stump, whittling with his switchblade.

"He's strong, that's for sure. We're gonna need the muscle," Stan says.

"You think he won't stab you in the back when he gets a chance? I've seen guys like him at Pendleton. Always got something to prove. Most of 'em have done time. You tell them, 'There's no *I* in *team*,' and they look at you like they're gonna rape your sister." He puts the last plate into the basket, leans closer to Stan. Sound is distorted by the slosh in the barrel, the incoming tide. "Where do you want to be when a guy like that's got a weapon in his hands?"

"I hear you," says Stan.

"Understand?" Cut again to Shaneequio whittling, footage from two days earlier that someone spliced in.

"I hear you," says Stan.

What he'd felt in the cave was bigger than the darkness, the eerie drawings, the guano. A stillness, a focus—he hasn't locked into it yet. But it reminded him of meditation, those too-rare moments when the noise drops away, the sense of yourself—the hardness of the floor, awareness of sounds, the feeling of being bound by a mortal sack of meat and viscera—starts to dissolve. He misses that feeling. Lately, when he tries to meditate, he is overwhelmed by the sense of himself. He can see himself standing on that Washington beach, face raised toward the sky. He can hear the shriek he'd held back, imagine himself doubling over and collapsing, rocking himself on the hard ground. A vision so pathetic it jolts him right out of his quiet, Ujayyi breathing gone to shit, squeezing and squeezing the stone in his pocket to keep from kicking something.

"There's a long game to be played," Bernatelli tells Stan. Candy trots up and puts her hands over Bernatelli's eyes, but the ex-Marine doesn't flinch.

"Guess who?" she says.

"Hey, guys, I think I see another bottle," someone cries off-camera. Shaneequio wipes the blade of his knife on his shorts, closes it with a sinister look. Stratus clouds speed overhead. Gloria Hamm sits splay-legged in the sand, peeling a lemon; she squints toward the waterline but stays where she is, missing another opportunity to get in the game. The APs are growing annoyed at her lack of initiative. The producer has counseled patience, but privately he worries that the dental hygienist is hopeless, a write-off.

"Come on, guess!" says Candy.

"Heidi Klum?" Bernatelli says in a bored voice. He pulls her hands away. "Oh, it's you."

The bolt from the crossbow had grazed Clarice's cheek, opening a nasty but shallow gash that drenched her tank top and painted her hands like a scene from a slasher movie. Richard fainted at the sight of it, falling eight feet out of the tree in which he'd been hiding, his own crossbow clattering to the ground and firing a bolt straight into the air. Somehow they don't have the shooter on tape—the field team was focused on Clarice, the hotheads and spycams all looking the wrong way. Once the chaos and jostling ended, the others clustered around Clarice in postures of panic and disbelief. Simon, the poet, shredded his T-shirt for bandages. Candy poured the contents of her canteen over Richard's face. Bernatelli and Stan watched from the far side of the clearing while Shaneequio, who had been huddled in the blind with Clarice, stalked the perimeter, flicking his switchblade open and closed. Casting policy aside, an A2 jumped into the shot and tried to give Clarice mouth-to-mouth. That A2 is now unemployed.

The producer rewinds the edited segment. "It's just a scratch," Clarice says, holding a sopping bandage to her face. Her Texas twang is growing stronger by the day. "I've got worse breaking a horse on granddad's ranch."

Had it been deliberate? Had Bernatelli really gotten Stan to take the shot? And if so, had the target been Shaneequio, or Simon, who lay just beyond the blind, a shrub strapped to his head for camouflage? From what the producer can see, examining the ISO feeds at more angles and speeds than the Zapruder film, it's impossible to know.

But what does it matter? Who cares who fired the shot, or at whom? By the end of the week it will have been resequenced, the audio sweetened, the lighting recast to create the right mood. They'll add an incriminating flashback, stolen shots in slo-mo, until they've created the story they want to tell—and to hell with what really happened. "What really happened gets about a four share," Armand used to say, in those long, boozy process meetings. The producer had disagreed. For five seasons this creative tension made for great television, the editing limited to pacing issues, camera angles, profanity. After Benin, however, the need to be more proactive had been impressed upon them. The crew was to shape reality, not vice versa. The lawyers made it absolutely clear.

And the producer has taught his team well. If it moved the story forward, there was no one who couldn't be the shooter: not Richard, semi-conscious in a bed of ferns; not Shaneequio, stabbing his knife into a tree trunk; not even Gloria, sitting glumly on a boulder, watching the others minister to Clarice. More troubling, there's no one who *wouldn't* be the shooter, if they thought it would raise their profile, separate them from the pack.

Though no one would buy Gloria Hamm as the shooter.

There she is again, he thinks. What is it that draws his attention to her? She seems uninterested in what happens to the others or to herself. She rarely talks, never seeks out the camera, never tries to upstage anyone. She's a stranger to the gratuitous insult; she doesn't flirt, threaten, or kvetch. He's seen the viewer-response data, seen Paco and Miley wince when she comes on screen. In daily meetings, her name hardly comes up. The storyboards don't look good at all.

"Better shape up, kid," he breathes.

On the live cam, the Deserted are getting ready for sleep. Tomorrow they'll leave the beach for good, driven into the woods by the latest advances in remote climate management. But they don't know that yet. For now, it's a peaceful night, the ocean translucent, the horizon an inkblot of blue clouds. At the water's edge, backlit by the crackling fire, Hiroko stands with hands clasped, chin high, and starts to sing.

"When you wish upon a star, makes no difference who you are . . ."

Her voice starts out shy, reedy, but slowly gains confidence, turning sultry and operatic.

"Anything your heart desires will come to you . . ."

Richard claps enthusiastically. Simon and Alejandra lie side by side like siblings, smiling distantly at the sound of the postal worker's voice. Bernatelli appraises the singer with narrowed eyes.

Clarice touches the thick bandage on her cheek. "Who does she think she is?" she whispers to Candy.

Candy glowers. "Seriously. What show does this bitch think she's on?"

"Look up," says the producer.

But no one looks up. They all watch Hiroko, the campfire's reflection digitally enhanced in nine pairs of eyes. Later, he'll watch her in the makeshift shower, her nipples hard in the glistening splash, her back perfectly arched as if she were in a shampoo commercial. But for now, the muscles of her neck as she belts out the song are enough, the purest quiver of her wind-chapped lips.

"Like a bolt out of the blue, fate steps in and sees you through . . ." Hiroko spreads her arms and the clouds draw apart, as though charmed by her song. There's real passion in her voice, a nightclub singer's va-va-voom.

A wolf-whistle from the campfire. "How about some rock and roll?" cries Stan. *"You can leave your hat on . . ."* he wheezes.

Even Shaneequio cracks a smile.

"What, from Miss Priss?" says Candy.

"Oh, cut her some slack," says Simon.

"Go fuck yourself, you little pussy," Candy says. "Go write a poem."

The scene devolves into insults and grumbles. Tomorrow someone will dig up a shot of Alejandra, or Candy, or maybe Shaneequio, face wet from the ocean, or the rain, or someone else's spit. They'll drop it into the sequence, a perfect cut from Hiroko's plaintive song to the Deserted's heartfelt response.

No one looks at the sky. They bicker and make obscene gestures until Bernatelli restores order. No one notices when the first stars emerge between tattered clouds, constellations never before observed by man or woman, created specially, and at great expense, with algorithms developed in Cupertino.

"You got to go back to the Second Great Migration, when these neighborhoods were at the threshold of the middle class," Shane-equio says. He and Candy stroll down the waterline, the gang counselor limping gingerly, the dazzlingly blonde lawyer listening with great solemnity. "Then you got manufacturing decline, white flight . . . After the riots, insecurity makes people territorial. You offer them protection, you win their loyalty, feel me? Enter the Crips."

"I don't think so, Patel," Miley says, throwing the director a look. The shot changes. She turns back to the producer. "Bernatelli's really showing lead in the old pencil. Look at that package. Can we get him in bicycle shorts somehow?"

Morning of day twelve, the Deserted are weary but undaunted, despite endemic sunburn and a diet winnowed to strips of dried squirrel meat and small, burned manioc cakes. The ocean is restless, the sky perfectly clear—for the moment.

An intern sets a pot of decaf on the producer's console. The morning shift circles through the command center with workmanlike lassitude. Patel goes over the shooting script with the remote camera operators. Video techs finish white balancing, while the chyron master amuses himself by morphing stills of the Deserted's faces into zoo animals. Taylette is in the galley, showing the interns the tattoo on the small of her back.

"Vegas has him out by Week Four. You buy that?" Miley says.

"Could be."

She scoffs. "Get real! If Bernatelli's not in the finale, I will totally blow you. *That's* how confident I am."

"We set for the electrical?" the producer says. He punches up the night's medicals—calorie intakes, core temps, blood pressure, electrolytes—scalds his tongue on the coffee. Hiroko has been running a fever for days, most likely a urinary tract infection; Shaneequio has brought up the rear since losing the hot-coal-walking contest. But it's Simon, the poet, who's in real trouble—sleeping 3.3 hours a night, food intake almost nonexistent, his wound visibly festering. His agent has been notified of the situation. She has insisted he stay on the show.

"You call Boby back yet?" Miley says with careful nonchalance, dialing through night footage: Richard propped on an elbow and staring at Bernatelli, scribbling in a journal with a devious look; Alejandra huddling between the roots of a banyan, sobbing in silent convulsions, her hair strung miserably in front of her face. The junior AP makes some notes, types in a couple of requests, sends the whole file to the editing server. Then turns a questioning eye to the producer.

"You talk to him," the producer says.

"He said he has some ideas—"

"I don't want to hear about it," he says. He can sweat that little hipster as well as the next guy. "Tell Boby whatever you have to tell him."

"That's not necessarily the best career strategy," Miley says, crossing her arms, subtly hefting her tits. "At this point, I mean."

"For whom?"

It's not a fair question. The thing about Miley is that she seems perfectly content in her job. He's worked with dozens of APs, all of whom regularly and abjectly demonstrated their devotion—but their slavering was always laced with hostility, the subtle suggestion that one day they'd happily butcher him in his sleep. For that reason, he knew how to keep an eye on them. But Miley seems to relish the role of lieutenant, even take pride in it. Sometimes he catches her watching him with something that could almost be admiration. It's unnerving.

"The electrical," he says.

Miley sucks her teeth, pulls out her walkie. "Weather, what's up with the storm?"

A crackling voice. "Stand by! Thunderheads generating in five." At the glare-bleached horizon, the sky starts to darken, pixel by pixel, shadows on a flawless ocean.

His father would have approved of the command center: the perfect ergonomics, the excruciating thought put into every aspect of the design, from the plasma monitors to the leather seats to the nonconducting rubber flooring to the volume controls in the head, conveniently located above the toilet paper dispenser. Over thirteen seasons they've perfected the floor plan: the arc of camera controls at the base of the monitors; a multitiered technical sector crowded with waveform monitors and vectorscopes, beetling with engineers and VTR ops; the "Audio Empire" on a raised platform to one side. And presiding over it all, an inner circle that houses the director and technical director, the APs, and the producer himself.

"A man needs the proper instrument," his father always said. For thirty-six years he'd sold hammers—but he hated the word "tool." "Give a man a tool and he'll get the job done. A man has the right *instrument*, he makes a work of art." The command center, with its virtual tentacles that sprawl across the island, across oceans, is the producer's instrument, he's often thought—each cut, each unexpected camera angle is a musical scale, each storybeat contributing to the long arc of the season like notes in an arpeggio. For twelve seasons he's played this instrument like a virtuoso, the show his multimedia magnum opus, a symphony dedicated to the very idea of "reality."

His father had traveled the Southwest with a steel display case full of beautifully designed hammers. He knew every mom-and-pop hardware store from Elko to El Paso. He dropped dead of an aneurysm in a motel outside Tucson. No one found him for a day and a half. The producer was living in Venice Beach then, twenty-three years old, waiting tables, taking acting classes. When he told his acting coach he had to skip a week to go to the funeral, the coach actually teared up. Then he said, "Take notes."

"Anyway, I think it's going fine," he tells Miley. He peers over the coffee mug at her bare feet, the silver ring on her middle right toe, her camo pants that fit tight as a mango skin. She catches him staring. "Don't let me interrupt you," she says.

"The Candy-Bernatelli thing works, Clarice and Alejandra have their secret little alliance, Stan is a perfect train wreck . . . Richard winning the hot coals was a boost—"

"Ree-*shard* . . ."

"Not everything has to be spectacular right out of the gate," he says. "Does Boby want everyone to set themselves on fire in the first segment? Things have to develop slowly; *that's* the real challenge. That's what makes it art."

"What about her?"

He sets the coffee mug down precisely in the ring it left on the console. "Who?"

Miley's smile is thin; she unconsciously runs a fingertip over the scar. "You get it, right? You know if this season isn't a game changer we're finished?" The producer watches Candy and Shaneequio gathering firewood, Bernatelli taking what appears to be a difficult shit. In the galley, one of the story assistants has dropped his pants to show Taylette his own tattoo. Patel, struggling with a mild bout of dysentery, calls cameras in a weak, pleading voice.

"We can't afford someone who doesn't do anything," Miley says. "Who doesn't say a word, doesn't start trouble. I'm trying to look out for you here. There's no room in the models for someone—"

"Maybe we should make room."

On Camera Six, Gloria Hamm, truculent and blunt of movement, shaves bark from eucalyptus trees, filling a canvas sack with tinder. Her medicals are flawless: she's eating well, sleeping close to seven hours, blood pressure basically unchanged. Her apathy is unrelenting, as though her body had no idea it was stranded on a remote island, as though it thought it was back in Garden City, getting ready for the day's appointments: flossing, scraping, the old brush-and-rinse. After two weeks the producer has started to see this as a kind of provocation.

"There's something about her," he says.

Paco struts in, to a sprinkle of applause and high fives. Last night he cleaned everyone out in Hold 'Em, dethroning Angela from Accounting, the standing champion. Afterward, he went to Angela's room and showed her how to win the money back. The exploits of El Lobo are the stuff of legend in Burbank. Boby's assistant has compiled a highlights reel.

"Buenos días, Bossman," Paco says with a smart salute. He stands next to Miley and stares at her pants. "Hola, mamacita. Remember our date? Today's el Día del Lobo."

Miley looks around as though not sure where the tiny sound came from. She turns back to the producer. "It's your show. Just let me know when you want, you know, my *assistance*."

He busies himself by punching up the blueprints for the Ancient Ruins. "That fucking sundial working yet?" he says to no one in particular.

"I'll be back," says Miley. "Gotta go see a guy about a monkey. Need anything?"

The "guy" is Hector, the new engineer-in-charge, the "monkey" a line or two of blow and Hector's uncircumcised cock. The producer has watched Hector and Miley fucking three, four times since preproduction. It's surprisingly boring. He'd always pegged Miley for a screamer. Sadly: no.

She pads away, cracks open the door of the command center. Sunlight glares out the monitors. "No one's saying she's not a nice, interesting person," she says. "You wouldn't be mixing that up with what the show needs, would you?"

"Who?" says Paco.

"Tall, dark, and moody over there." Gloria Hamm has put down the bag of bark and stands watching the darkened horizon, leaning slightly forward on the balls of her feet. Last night the producer meditated before his monitors, the image of Gloria's face frozen there like a mandala.

Paco laces his hands behind his head and shows the grin that earned him his nickname. "Coño, some strong legs on that one. Think about the vice grip—"

"Shut up," says the producer.

While the Deserted go about their tasks, here comes Gloria: eyes alert, nostrils widening at the change in the air. There's heavy weather on the way, dangerous enough to put their camp at risk. Who will react first? Who has the reflexes to save the Deserted?

At the first growl of thunder she takes off down the beach, snatches clothing off the line, drags the foot locker of squirrel meat under the tarp. The horizon cramps with charcoal; the first wicked thread of lightning throws the camp into relief. Bernatelli and Candy, caught lounging in a tide pool, sprint stumbling toward the others; the Marine lifts Simon to his feet and helps him into the shelter, just as a muscular bolt bursts the top of a palm tree into flame.

"See what I mean?" Miley says. "That man's not going anywhere. Don't forget our bet."

The producer waves her off. "Save it for Hector."

With the drag and point of a mouse, five more palm trees explode. The producer sips his coffee. The image of Gloria had quieted his mind for a time, but after meditation he was more keyed up than before. Something in her eyes—some lightlessness, or absence—it would not let him sleep.

"You're a tool," he'd told his father once, during some adolescent argument. It was the worst thing he could think to throw at him. He'd expected a smack in the face, but the old man just coughed out a laugh.

"Now you're getting it," he said.

In the beginning there was the idea, a passionate if inchoate sense of mission with which they descended from Armand's roof, ready to do battle with higher-ups, armed only with a process message that, looking back, was audaciously vague: *Viewers will see what it is like to be other people. They will learn the truth of the human heart and mind.*

From idea to pitch, then a string of meetings in which the suits were frankly uncomprehending but intrigued. Free will: a concept of such beautiful simplicity no one quite knew how to discuss it. You chose the environment, replete with its own challenges, dropped the unsuspecting players into it, and left them alone. No host, no gags, no idiotic games. And no intervention. It would be unpredictable, risky. "That's what makes it real," Armand said. He had the bad taste to bring up Godard, which almost sank the whole meeting. But when they pointed out how much they'd save in casting and postproduction costs, the suits raised their eyebrows and leaned back in their chairs.

"We're thinking of calling it *Abandoned!* With an exclamation mark," the producer said. The suits frowned. "We're not married to it," he said.

They'd had to leverage every ounce of Armand's reputation, but in the end they got everything they wanted. Six months later they were in the Everglades, sweating their asses off, watching ten exhausted strangers learn to hate each other, their manners and habits unraveling into atavism. A year later all the networks were trying to copy what they'd done. There were licensed clones of the show in eight countries.

But now their revolution is in trouble, their innovations passé. Once upon a time people had wanted an unfiltered window into the lives of their fellow men and women, a mirror held up to the world. Sure, that mirror had to be adjusted, the window tinted, a nudge here, an edit there, to reel the story in—reality, after all, is infinite and ever changing; television, by contrast, is all too finite. You needed to schedule your spots with some degree of accuracy. But the idea! The idea had been sound. Now the market is flooded with crude gimmicks, ever-more-extravagant rewards. The mirror is warped beyond recognition. In its spare simplicity the idea has come to seem priggish, as quaint as the original working title. Little by little they've let the network introduce "innovations" to bring the show in line with the competition. But how can the producer compete with shows about extreme sex reassignment, public transit sabotage, hunger strike contests? A source in Burbank says Boby is developing an Ultimate Fighting show featuring spouses with a history of domestic violence. Before such spectacle, such degrada-tion, the producer feels helpless, a dinosaur. Even the blogs have turned against him. "THE END IS NEAR!" they're screaming on TMZ. "Will the network desert *The Deserted*?" They'd gotten the green light for the new season, but everyone can sense a reckoning coming, a new paradigm taking shape: postreality, though no one can yet say what that means.

"I guess we're on our own," says Candy, in the edited, post-storm sequence. "Guess we have to start over."

"That's some coldhearted shit," Shaneequio says, standing over what's left of the shelter. "Gonna be rough on Simon now, no roof over his head."

"Stop complaining," Bernatelli says. "We've got work to do." He and Shaneequio face off. Alejandra sits in the sand and whimpers. Stan trembles against a tree, eyes wide with shock.

"Should I call his agent?" Taylette said during the taping, nodding at the catatonic Arkansan.

"Not yet," the producer said.

The camp is wrecked, the shelter torched by flaming palm fronds, crushed by a stray aileron that the wind flipped up the beach. The editors have thrown together a good montage of the storm's aftermath: Candy and Bernatelli salvaging wood; Clarice combing small crustaceans out of Alejandra's hair while the math teacher weeps into her hands; Hiroko and Richard huddling around Simon, who shivers in what's left of the blankets, face pale as a corpse, his wounded leg dark gray and rubbery. Gloria trails at the perimeter, picking up clothing, the group's only compass, a few sand-coated scraps of squirrel meat.

"Gotta get rid of someone, Boss," Paco said. "I vote for the dentist. Call me crazy." The producer pretended not to hear.

"There's always Simon," said Miley. "He's on his last leg." Groans from the story editors. Interns laughed politely.

"What about one of the healthy players?" said Patel. "Why do we always single out the defenseless?"

"Uh, because they can't defend themselves?" suggested the chyron master.

Now, watching from his quarters, the producer sits in full lotus, presses his palms to the hardwood, and lifts himself off the floor. Bernatelli tears a strip of denim from a blackened pair of jeans, ties it around his head Rambo-style. "Buck up, people," he barks. "This is just the beginning. Or the end of the beginning. Never say die."

"Easy for you to say," says Hiroko, stroking Simon's forehead. "You not have gangrene." Alejandra looks at Simon's pale face, at Bernatelli looming over them, and cries harder. Cut to Stan Clewes, hunched on a charred log, staring blank-faced out to sea.

"At least now we can build a nicer shelter," says Richard with forced jollity. "I hated the old one. Not enough color. And the feng shui was all wrong."

Bernatelli stands before the group. "I know you're tired. I know it's been a hard day. But let me tell you all something—"

"When the going gets tough," the producer mutters.

"When the going gets tough," Bernatelli says. The producer settles back to the floor and hits mute.

With each passing season he grows less convinced of the Deserted's reality, of their basic humanity. They're cardboard cutouts, the personas they develop ever more elaborate and yet more predictable. Miley calls it "televolution," the way their personalities hew ever closer to those of previous seasons and other shows, their triumphs, failures, love affairs, betrayals converging like images in an elevator mirror. And they're happy to do it: They're killing each other for the opportunity. No humiliation or discomfort is too much. The sex-changers, the mothers who beat their children on camera, the couples who document their own ugly divorces, the husbands who screw their secretaries, the wives who screw their trainers, the secretaries who screw their bosses' wives. Cinemax's new show follows a group of high school girls in a contest to give the most blow jobs on a summer trip to Europe. Hookers turned kindergarten teachers, housewives turned hookers, drug dealers turned Christian marriage counselors. Whole families cooking up publicity stunts in their garages. Prison inmates rioting with story outlines in their back pockets. The worse it gets, the longer the lines at casting calls, the more frantically the websites and Page Six items proliferate. It's been a long time since *The Wrecking Ball*, when they'd knock on someone's door and offer her a new home.

"It's like they're writing it for us," the producer tells Armand. "Who taught them to do that?"

"Why, you did, dear," says Armand. "We both did."

They're quiet a moment, distant strains of mariachi music coming through the phone. "Do you know what happened last night?" the producer asks.

"Tell me there was a gang bang."

"Simon spontaneously started reciting poetry. *Shakespeare*, for fuck's sake. The guy's half dead—"

"He is a poet . . ."

"Sure he is," the producer says, unfolding his legs. The trailer feels chilly, though the thermostat reads a balmy 80 degrees. "How would I know if he's really a poet? How would anyone know? He could be an astrophysicist. He could be a plumber . . ."

"Who on earth would pretend to be a poet?"

"I'm just saying, they're all playing roles. They're being the people they think we want them to be." The music is getting louder, the plaintive strains of a lovesick singer. They still serenade in San Miguel, Armand says. The men still stand below their beloved's window and pour out their souls, despite the millions who've done it before. "It was supposed to be about unpredictability," the producer says. "Remember? About how different people are. It's depressing."

"There's this lovely café just off the main square," says Armand. "Have I told you? No lattés or soy chai—just coffee. The loveliest umbrellas, tables right on the sidewalk. I sit there all afternoon, sometimes, and at four o'clock the vocational school across the street lets out, all these young men in black pants, white button-down shirts, twenty, twenty-one . . ." The music comes closer, Armand puts down the phone—the producer can hear him waving off the band. *Gracias*, he says. *Mas tarde.* "Anyway, it makes me happy just watching."

"Up to your old tricks," the producer says, flicking the sound back on.

"Just watching." There had been the scandal, many years ago, Armand and three network pages at his Lake Tahoe condo. There had been a string of heartbreaks, incidents in restaurants, one nuisance suit by a prostitute Armand swears he never met. "What can I tell you," he sighs. "I'm very predictable."

On the island, night is deepening, the stunned faces of the Deserted fading to shadow. From the dark interior comes the lonesome howl of a coyote. It's the same coyote that howled across the Steppe, the same coyote that stalked the Deserted through the Tetons. It might have howled in the frozen wilderness of Antarctica, had the producer and Paco not had a brief and pointed discussion.

The Deserted sit side by side on a charred log, staring at the ocean, a palm tree still sizzling behind them. You can almost smell the ozone. "You hear the one about the Jew, the queer, and the nigger in a rowboat?" says Bernatelli.

"Fuck you say?" Shaneequio groans, but can't muster the strength to get up. Hiroko giggles. Richard glares murderously. Alejandra sobs. Stan Clewes still stares blankly, his jaw clicking open and shut. The shot draws back, the Deserted shrinking to a pale line before the dark forest. The sky has cleared to a sad, nacreous indigo, spattered with brilliant stars in intricate patterns. Somewhere in those patterns are coded directions to the Ancient Ruins. Tomorrow, or the next day, the Deserted will arrive at the sacred site where temples once stood to the god Xiolticanqatzl. With their bare hands and whatever tools they can fashion, they'll excavate shards of pottery, jewelry, caches of modern toiletries, packaged meals created by Wolfgang Puck. Buried somewhere in the ruins is a human skull—whoever finds it will spend a night in the Isolation Chamber of Xiolticanqatzl. There's a hidden tomb where the winning team will find a sarcophagus full of gold coins, courtside tickets to the Final Four, written instructions for the journey to the Volcanic Labyrinth. The island's real inhabitants had no written language. Their gods were animals and mountains that had no proper names. Paco and Hector invented Xiolticanqatzl one night during preproduction, stoned out of their minds. Some Peruvian anthropologist did the sketches.

"Look up," says the producer. No one looks up.

The stars had been Miley's idea, an ambitious deal with Pixar that involved points on the show's syndication, *Making Of . . .* rights, and generous advertising for *WALL•E III*.

If they already know what's expected of them, why pay consultants to build the perfect cast? You could scoop ten people off the street, and soon they'd be forming cabals, plotting revenge, making threats, performing fellatio, sobbing on cue, and generally exhibiting the range of trite, selfish behavior audiences can't get enough of. You didn't have to create the Deserted: just give people a chance to express the Deserted they already wanted to be. What need for storyboards or imagination? Where's the art?

And if there's no art, who needs an artist?

"Look up, dumbasses," he says.

He closes his eyes, squeezes the stone until his forearm aches. When he opens them, there's Gloria, caught unawares by a sandcam as she picks something out of her teeth. What role is she playing? Who has she decided to be? The producer has no idea.

After an eternity, she lets out a sigh and turns away from the others. While he holds his breath, Gloria leans back in the sand and at last lifts her face to the lovely, perilous sky.

WEEK THREE

■

After fifteen days on the island, the Deserted are at each other's throats. Food is growing scarce, and tempers are strained to the breaking point. The shelter was destroyed by a freak thunderstorm that tested their fragile relationships. Messages in the stars sent them charging into the jungle—but no one can imagine the challenges that await them at the Ancient Ruins. Simon's gangrene is spreading. Stan Clewes is still unresponsive. Candy and Bernatelli still look like a power couple, destined to lead. *Not so fast*, says Alejandra, whose father was a Marine and lost an arm in Vietnam. And what about Shaneequio, whose jealousy is heating up? Don't count him out. Richard decided his best strategy is to flirt with Bernatelli, to get under the leader's skin and provoke him to do something rash. No one knows what Gloria Hamm thinks about anything. Six months after his father's death, the producer had a panic attack while walking on the beach. For almost a year, he couldn't go near the ocean without a cold grip seizing his heart and making the world seem strange and dangerous. He lost a bit part he'd landed on *Melrose Place* and took a job as a production assistant.

He couldn't know how that decision would change everything, just as the ten players can't foresee the bruising trials still ahead on the path to Paradise. But their wills are unbowed, their eyes wide open. It's Week Three, the drama's just getting started, and the island has lots of surprises in store for the Deserted . . .

They come at dawn, creeping from the shadows like liquid spirits of the island itself. Two from the jungle, two from the ocean, two rappelling down from the canopy, all in black. Once in position, they send text messages to the team leader, who transmits the code for ALL READY to the Facility; within seconds all recording cameras and microphones go dark, the moonlight dims, the roar of the ocean rises to cover the sound of their approach. The message comes back from the Facility: PROCEED.

For three days he has not spoken or eaten, not shown any expression beyond a vacuous stare. He doesn't swim, doesn't bathe. If another player leads him by the elbow he follows, but he'll go nowhere of his own accord, just sit on a log through heat and cold and any kind of weather. He did not participate in the Sand Castle Design Extravaganza, had nothing to say during the other night's Truth Telling to Hiroko. Even Bernatelli has been unable to elicit a response from his erstwhile ally. Yesterday, while the others set traps for the small, grouse-like birds that suddenly seem to be everywhere, Bernatelli had Candy flash her breasts—but Stan hardly blinked, a thin line of spittle dribbling from his mouth. It was the last straw. The blogs are up in arms ("If this was Antartica [*sic*] some one wd have shoved this boring fuck into a crevace allready!"—*DesertedWatch.com*); *TV Guide* has summed it up with the poisonous headline: "CLEWES-LESS!"

When the extraction team enters the new shelter—a distinct

improvement over the old, featuring chintz curtains and a crude hot tub—some of the Deserted awaken and prop themselves up to watch. No one has had to tell them what's coming—they know instinctively what awaits those who fail to contribute to the show. Their faces are grim, resigned; this is a reminder to them all, a lesson in the truth of their situation: Stop moving and die.

With ruthless precision the shadows converge on Stan, who lies fetal at the back of the shelter, eyes open and tracking their approach. When a hand reaches for his arm, he scurries to one side, where more shadows wait with a straitjacket and cloth hood printed with the network logo. There are thuds and grunts, a long, shaky cry; Stan shambles to his feet, shoulders one assailant into a support beam. Another takes a vicious kick in the balls.

"Ouch," says Audio.

"Fuck me," says Paco, resting both hands in his groin.

"No. *No!*" Stan shrieks, the first words he's spoken since the thunderstorm. "*I'll eat, okay? I'll eat!*" The extraction team works him into a corner while the rest of the Deserted scramble out of the way. Richard, trembling in nightshirt and cap, hides behind Bernatelli; Alejandra, not realizing the cameras are off, starts weeping again, turning so the early light catches her tears. "*No, please! Please, Jesus!*" says Stan as they drag him inch by inch toward the sand. "*Don't fuckin' touch me! No no no . . .*" He manages to wrap both arms around a corner post, kicking furiously with both feet. "*Walter!*" he shouts, but Bernatelli stands impassive, jaw clenched: He's a soldier; he understands that in war, some men don't come home. The extraction team pauses, regroups, then pounces as one on the hapless Arkansan, fists surging mercilessly at all his soft body parts. It takes only seconds to immobilize his legs, and then he is yanked toward the door; when he still clings to the corner post, a precision kick breaks one of his arms with an audible crack.

"Guess that's what you call 'southern discomfort,'" says Paco, taking a ten-dollar bill from the chyron master. "I told you, man: It's in the eyes. El Lobo sees all."

"Third fucking season in a row," says the chyron master. "People gonna start thinking the fix is in, Lobo."

"Yeah," says Audio. "This is some clear-cut intervention and shit!"

"Nah," Paco says, with a wink at Patel. "Bossman don't believe in that."

The producer doesn't take the bait. "We're doing a call with Boby tomorrow," he tells the APs, who ignore him.

A perfect, ominous shot from behind of Stan being escorted back to the beach, three dark figures on either side. He wears the strait-jacket, the hood with the network logo; his head turns side to side, listening for some indication that his companions will rescue him. They will not. Stan Clewes is going home.

"Good riddance," says Miley, typing a message to the extraction team. "We'll need to explain that broken arm to Legal."

"Tell 'em the black guy did it!" says an engineer.

"Could be Clarice," Paco suggests. "Retaliation for the crossbow thing."

"Will he be taken to a doctor?" Patel says.

Camera Two says, "Say he was jacking off too much. Got the hots for Bernatelli and couldn't control himself."

"I think that's called 'projection,'" says Taylette. The other cameras snicker.

"People," says the producer. Hotheads and ISO cams come back on, and the rest of the Deserted go about their morning—stirring mush in a tin pot, washing their faces in the sea with all the refreshing glamour of a Nivea spot, eyeing one another in speculation: Who will be next? The team marches their pathetic captive up the trail to Beachhead B, where a skiff waits to take him to the network ship for processing, then on to Bangkok, Dubai, Frankfurt,

New York. He's the 109th player to leave the show—and not even remotely the most endearing. Still, the image gives the producer an unexpected pang. He almost feels for the guy.

"I heard his agent did a deal with Bravo for a cooking show," Taylette says.

"I heard that, too!" says a story assistant. "A spinoff of *Top Chef*. They're calling it *Roadkill Café*."

"Man," says Paco, "think pendejo will get to work with Padma? Maybe El Lobo oughtta go catatonic."

"Angela says you already did," says Audio, to hoots and cries.

"The call?" the producer says. "How about everyone start figuring out what we're going to tell Boby."

"What *we* are going to tell Boby?" Patel says, and shoots Paco a look. Patel came on last season, the fourth director to fill the chair originally occupied by Sandy Beers. He's quiet and finicky, never socializes with the others. He spends most of his free time talking to his wife in Covina. During preproduction the producer constantly had to send runners to drag Patel off the phone. Eventually they had to have a conversation.

The extraction feed has been banished to a corner of the monitor wall. The producer watches Stan step gingerly into the skiff, shoulders slumped in defeat. There will be no trace of this sequence in the show that airs; the remaining Deserted will be briefed on a suitable exit narrative. The footage will be sequestered in Burbank, evaluated by industrial psychologists, our extraction procedures further refined.

Miley finishes typing, scans her laptop. "Next up, the ruins," she says. "Everyone see the footage from last night?" She brushes back a strand of hair and the producer catches another glimpse of the scar, raised and pink, shaped like a cartoon thunderbolt. She sticks out her tongue. The producer frowns.

"Told you the math teacher would crack the star code," Paco says.

"Looks like homegirl bought herself another week." Audio fakes a dramatic yawn. Camera Three sniffles, rubs imaginary tears from his eyes. "No chinga a la latina, motherfuckers," Paco says. "My girl's got game."

"*Your* girl?" says Taylette.

"Jealous?" says an intern; when Taylette turns to him he blanches.

Clarice, face still wadded with bandages of seaweed, confers with Richard about the lack of hot water in the hot tub. "I'll tell ya, sweet thing, more fuel'n a Texas barbecue pit round here. Where's it all goin'?" Cut to a shot of Gloria blowing on the cooking fire, heating up an illicit extra pot of mush; cut to Bernatelli, Candy, Hiroko, and the others hard at work building the new shelter. At the edge of camp, dozens of the small gray birds jostle and scrounge in the dirt.

"Can somebody please figure out where those damn birds are coming from?" the producer says. "They're messing with the calorie count." A couple of story assistants wrestle over a laptop, while Paco and Miley review assignments for the Ancient Ruins. Sensing a lull, the producer squats next to Patel's chair like a golfer discussing a putt.

"I need to do a location survey," he says quietly. "In the Ballard Zone. Think you could take a group? There's this cave."

"A cave?"

"Just an idea I've got. Not even an idea. A hunch. Can you help me out? And keep it quiet for now."

Patel stares straight ahead, working his tongue around the inside of his mouth. Across the floor, Miley shoves Paco, who'd been sticking his nose dangerously close to her ear. "Do they—"

"No," the producer says. "Not yet. I want to kick it around in my head first, see what's possible. Look, I'd appreciate it."

"Can you please get off her backside, Camera One!" Patel says.

Camera One waves dismissively without turning around, but the shot of Candy widens out. Patel looks down at the producer. "Is it a cave or a mine entrance?"

"How should I know?"

Patel reaches for a plastic binder by his feet. "There are quite a few mine entrances in the mountains," he says, opening it to a photocopied map. "Many of the shafts were never sealed. There would be insurance issues, I think."

"Right. Leave that side of it to me. I just want to take a look. Take an engineer," he says, quickly adding, "but not Hector."

"Have you read any of the research about this island? It's quite interesting." He flips through the binder, considers a page, flips again. "This was one of the largest nickel mining operations in the world. Did you know? Look at these figures. From 1980 to 1985 alone they mined close to $800 million. That's today's dollars. And that's not including copper. There was also cobalt and gold, in the interior." The producer squints at the binder. "Coco has old maps and records," Patel says. "There are so many things we don't know. The natives—"

"Terrific," says the producer. He couldn't give less of a shit about nickel, but if it brings Patel on board, he's willing to look at a pie chart.

"It could be an interesting part of the show," Patel says, "if we can find a way to involve the Deserted. It's a very good story, if you would like—"

"Sounds like a hell of a story. How's day after tomorrow? I'll get Trish to cover."

Before he can answer, shouting breaks out at the video toaster. Techs are crowding behind the camera control units, and Audio shoves his way through the scrum.

"Let me see!" shouts the chyron master. "Move aside!"

"Oh, thank you, Jesus," cries Camera Two.

On the beach, Clarice stands nose to nose with Hiroko, red in the face, while the shy postal worker crosses her arms and tries to turn away. "Don't you walk away from me, bitch," says the systems analyst, grabbing Hiroko by the wrist. "I want you to tell me—we all got the right to know, dang it!"

"You no have right to know anything!" says Hiroko. "Let go me!"

"Did you fuck him or not, you little whore?"

At which Hiroko hauls back and, with surprising strength, smacks Clarice across her unbandaged cheek. The applause is deafening. There aren't enough rubber bands in the producer's cup to quiet the room.

"Ready to roll interview!" shouts Patel, but nobody hears him. "Hold the cross, Camera Four—what are you doing?" Shaking his head, the director pushes through the crowd to work the switcher himself.

"Go git her, girl!" Taylette says, as Clarice picks herself off the sand with a shriek of rage.

"Go for the bikini top! The bikini top!"

"Don't mess with Texas!"

"Score one for the U.S. Postal Service!" says Audio. Techs turn to him in confusion. "What?" he says.

The Deserted gather around the two women, some trying to separate them, some egging them on. It's a good old-fashioned girl fight—a strategic leak to YouTube will generate a week's worth of tabloid coverage, at least sixty seconds on *Access Hollywood*. With any luck, it might even get Coors back on board. Boby's probably beating off at his mahogany desk right now.

Clarice tackles Hiroko and they roll around the beach, sand dusting their skin in all the right places. Shaneequio and Bernatelli have, for once, stopped glaring at each other. Richard clutches his hair and shouts, "Ladies, please!" just as Hiroko gets a grip on the waist of Clarice's skirt and yanks the fabric away.

"Banzai!" says Audio.

"I can' hol' 'er, Cap'n!" cries the chyron master. "I'm takin' 'er to Boner Factor Three!"

Miley shakes her head and goes back to planning assignments for the Ancient Ruins. Paco holds up his arms like a referee signaling a touchdown.

It's chaos in the camp, a third-week coup. But back in the shelter, Gloria Hamm is suffering. The producer watches her monitor—red-eyed, her arms and legs swollen with an angry rash, the dental hygienist lies on her bedroll and scratches madly. She lifts her T-shirt to reveal a belly mapped with scabs. She grits her teeth and scratches between her legs, grunting like a ballplayer.

"I thought Enviro cleared all the poison oak," the producer says.

Miley glances at the ISO. "Guess not."

On the line monitor, a jug of suntan oil has broken, coating Clarice and Hiroko as they wrestle in the sand. "Take me now," says Camera Two, on his knees, face raised to the ceiling.

Gloria hauls herself to her feet and heads downhill toward the ocean. When she wades in, the producer can almost feel the sting of salt water. "Can't we do something?"

Miley closes her laptop. "You mean, *intervention*? I think someone said we don't do that here. I think someone said"—she drops her voice to a haughty baritone—"'This isn't the fucking *Hills*, people.'"

"I'm not talking about intervention. I'm talking about helping someone." Miley tilts her head. She's almost sympathetic. Whatever she says is drowned out by squeals of delight: Clarice and Hiroko have started to make out.

"Forget it," he mutters. With a last look at Gloria, he gets out of the chair and starts for his quarters. It's going to take a long meditation to prepare for tomorrow's conference call, for Boby's idiotic meddling. The heat in his trailer seems to be on the fritz and a refill of scented mist has not yet arrived from his yoga teacher. A low whimper follows him to the door of the command center, a sound of such pitiable desperation that he turns, expecting to see Gloria gouging at her skin.

Instead, there's a wide shot of the skiff and its passenger, adrift in an endless ocean. The sun throws a bright shaft miles wide. There are no landmarks—not the island, vanished in the distance, not the network ship, anchored miles ahead. The hazy sky, the glare on the water, make the skiff seem almost to be flying, sailing through the air, its lone passenger leaving the world behind. The producer holds the door handle, frozen by the sound of misery, stung by an inexplicable surge of guilt. A second later the image is gone, replaced by a shot of a monkey throwing nuts at the hilarious crowd.

"What I'm saying is, when we got into this we were all about 'no formulas,' but the whole no-formula thing's kind of turned into a formula, you dig?" Boby al-Hajj, senior VP of programming, has a habit of using obsolete slang in an effort to appeal to the older generation. "What I'm saying is, we need to reach consensus on some new ideas, some out-of-the-box shit, and in a hurry."

Miley flops her tanned, bug-bitten legs on the conference table, sucking on a Tootsie Pop loud enough for Boby to hear. Patel lies sleeping across the table, one dead arm just inches from the speakerphone, while Paco cleans his fingernails with a bamboo splinter, a copy of *Loving God with All Your Mind* open in front of him. Outside the hut, the jungle rustles, whistles, and shrieks.

"Listen to this," Paco says, swiveling his chair. "'Knowing God and trusting in His promise causes all things to work together for good.' Blah, blah . . . Okay: 'You never need to wonder about the events in your life.' Where's the drama in that?"

Miley ignores him. "Gotta stay organic, Boby my love," she says with a slurp. "Gotta see what happens here. Gotta ride it."

"No dice, sweet cheeks. Organic is tanking. When was the last time we were on *ET*? You reading the blogs? People have no idea what the show's *about*."

"It's about brain death," says Paco. "It's about what every show's about."

Miley frowns at Paco, squeezes her left breast and mouths, "Suck it."

The producer watches the speakerphone and silently repeats a mantra. From the east comes the roar of a lion, though the real lions don't arrive for another week.

Paco flips a page. "'You can respond to good or bad situations with faith that God is at work . . .'"

"Look kids," Boby says—never mind that he's almost twenty years younger than the producer—"the point is, if something doesn't happen, and fast, we're looking at the long good-bye. Or more like the short good-bye, you feel me?"

"What kind of thing?" the producer says.

"Chill," Miley says.

"What?" says Boby.

"What kind of thing? What are you talking about?"

"You're the producer, not me. Aren't you supposed to, like, produce?"

Everyone stares at the phone. Even Patel raises his head. The ground has begun to vibrate with the imminent elephant stampede. Overnight, Simon took a turn for the worse, his wounded leg now paralyzed and completely black. Candy suggested they smother him in his sleep. Shaneequio and Clarice nearly came to blows over a potato, and this morning Richard stole Bernatelli's shorts off the line and strutted around in them, sans underwear. Sixteen days in, and the Deserted are riddled with conflict, a level of volatility that once would have seemed over the top. But it's not enough for Boby.

"I'm just saying, G: You're in charge. It's all you, my man. And I know," says Boby, reverting to some motivational speech pattern picked up in B-school, "I *know* you'll come up with something. For instance, I'm talking to my peeps at Endeavor—"

"You want me to stab someone in their sleep? You want me to put cholera in their water sacs? What the fuck, Boby—"

"Cholera's messy," says Paco. "Maybe, like, dengue . . ."

"Shut it," Miley says.

"Free will!" the producer says, standing over the speaker, his mantra a distant, Sanskrit memory. "The whole point is for them to discover their own purpose, not for us to spell it out. Maybe we give hints—"

"Write messages in the stars," Miley says.

"—write messages in the stars, but they make their own choices. This isn't *Who Wants to Be a Heart Surgeon?* Go back and read the treatment."

"Am I in philosophy class?" Boby says. "Did I hire you to be, like, the network philosopher? I got a bottom line to worry about, homeboy."

"Did *you* hire me?"

"'You will stop trying to take matters into your own hands,'" Paco reads, pointing at each of them in turn, "'and trust God instead.'" The producer throws him a look of such malevolence that the AP literally jumps in his chair.

Boby says, "My homies at Endeavor think maybe a guest star, like a surprise appearance?"

"No."

"You remember that chick from *Everybody Loves Raymond?*"

Paco puts down the book. "The one with the tetas?"

"Boby, no. I'm drawing a line," he tells the speakerphone. "No guest stars, no intervention. Free will—*that's* what this show is about. That's the artistic vision."

From Burbank, the sound of a hand slapping a mahogany desk. "Fuck your line, and fuck your artistic vision, dude. You want to go back to panel shows?"

In the next moment the producer finds himself back in the chair, Miley straddling him, holding his arms to his sides. The speakerphone crackles hoarsely on the floor. Patel is moving papers and laptop computers out of danger.

"Boby, honey, maybe someone with some more pizzazz? Send me your ideas," Miley calls over her shoulder. An incoherent burst of static comes in reply. Paco tucks the book under his arm and leaves the hut, whistling. An elephant's majestic trumpet can be heard in the distance, followed by a bloodcurdling human scream. Followed by silence.

Later, walking back to his quarters, Miley says, "There are some things we can do. Might not hurt to let Boby have his way once in a while. You just have to let him think he's in charge."

"Is that what you have to do?"

Miley grins. "That and a beaver shot. Gotta love the leather mini."

Above the trees, the mountains are wreathed in fog, almost imaginary. He tries to recall the feeling of walking in those mountains: the clean sting of cold air, the quiet, the absolute presence of stone. In the other direction, transmitters and dishes sit atop a bare hill like toys jumbled out of a child's closet. This morning the island's receivers went down for thirteen seconds, every last one of them, blasting the command center with audio and video white noise. When the signal snapped back, Paco said, "Man, that was the best scene this week." Hector sent engineers to every corner of the island in search of the problem but found nothing.

"Not radical changes, just tweaks," she says. "You love the show, right? You want it to get the biggest audience it can. So you adjust, spice it up, broaden the appeal. The original idea's still there, the vision. It's just . . . more. You know this," she says. "You taught me."

"We're doing a fucking tango contest. How much spicier do you want?"

Miley stops, scuffs at the base of a tree with her toe. "You're going to have to take it down a notch," she says. Somewhere the image of her toe is being captured, her name flashing next to the tree's serial number. "Everyone knows we wouldn't be here without you. Everyone believes in what you're doing. Think I'd stick around otherwise?"

Boby's first official act was to offer Miley her own extreme cosmetics show. The producer had been incommunicado, lost in the Olympic forest; as he'd heard the story, Miley stormed into Boby's office and ripped up the offer sheet, and by the time she walked out the little prick had signed off on Season Thirteen. Now he can add to that tableau: miniskirt, beaver.

They're at the edge of the producer's private area, the air alive with the chatter of birds. "Things change, right? Reality doesn't sit still. You showed me that," she says. "Remember my first full season? I was all about micromanaging. But you showed me how to be patient and ride it, wait for the opportunity. I was blown away.

"But it's the *opportunity*, right?" she says. "There's a difference between patience and letting the pitch go by."

"You think I should intervene?"

She looks almost embarrassed, as though she wants to touch him in some caring way. "You trust me, right? You know I'm your man. What you want, I make happen—that's how it's always been. I'm just saying, keep an open mind. Let me talk to him about this guest thing, just to keep the heat off you for a while."

They sit on the stoop of his trailer and he stares at a cluster of bites on Miley's knee. *The show's whatever you say it is*, she'd said. He has no idea if it's still true.

"Is there anything going on I need to know about?" he says.

She looks at him steadily, too smooth to blink. "Like what?"

He reaches into his pocket, squeezes the small stone. He'd stood in the cave entrance and run his fingers over the crude drawings, trying to convince himself that people had actually lived there. Not for seven weeks, or seven years: forever. They'd slept and eaten and shit there, and if they got voted out they died. They didn't go hang out on Patpong Road for two weeks or do the rounds of talk shows: they stopped breathing, decomposed. Their mates, however hairy or stooped, huddled against the wall and wailed inconsolably. Did they ever wonder why? When cyclones hurled against the island, when their hunters were mauled by animals, when their babies died in the womb, did they ask who was responsible? Did they wonder who had put them there, and whether it was merely for sport, for entertainment? They must have attributed all of it to their gods, he thinks. How they must have loathed their gods.

"I don't know." He waves a hand in the direction of the Facility. "Nothing. It's those birds. They've got me all bent out of shape."

Miley leans back in the sunshine. "Hector says they might have come on the ships, you know, during Pre? Like an invasive species. No natural predators on the island, so they run wild." She wiggles her toes, brings one foot closer to examine the polish. "Kind of like us, right? You okay?"

He stares over her shoulder at the dim mountains. "Birds, poison oak, screwy weather—what's happening to this place?" he muses. "Sure," he says. "I'm fine." This morning Patel sent a spreadsheet detailing Ballard's annual profits over the five decades the company had owned the island. Before Ballard the island had been virtually untouched, only a smattering of aborigines and a colony of rare white gibbons. The field teams have dug up arrowheads, potsherds. "Maybe we can start a collection or exhibit?" Patel wrote in the email. "So the crew can feel more connected to their work. I'm happy to take the lead on this."

Another distant scream breaks the silence. To the north the Deserted are in full flight before the enraged elephants. Shaneequio has flung Simon over one shoulder, the poet unconscious and septic. Tomorrow, or the next day, he'll be on the skiff. Sooner or later they all will be.

"I can't stop thinking about Stan," he says.

Miley scoffs. "That hillbilly shitbag. You never heard about his callback, did you? You know Patricia, in casting? She was about to file sexual assault charges, then suddenly she gets six months paid vacation. I wouldn't feel too bad for Stan."

"You think that was really him?" He takes out the rock, holds it in his palm. The sun barely seems to touch it—just a solid, inert thing, absorbing the light, a little world unto itself. "Or just a character he decided to play?" The producer's wife had come into the bathroom one morning while he was on the toilet, a week before he was to leave for Nicaragua. "I met someone," she said, then sat on the tiles and cried, and what had gone through his mind was how long he had to sit there before he could politely wipe his ass.

"Does it matter?" Miley says. "That's how televolution works."

"I just wonder if *he* knows the difference."

The elephant stampede ends with a riot of trumpets, leaving an eerie quiet over the jungle. In their foxholes, on their high branches, the Deserted are breathing, eyes closed, blood hammering in their ears.

"Look," Miley says. "I've got story meeting. We've gotta block out Simon's endgame, and there are still some bad sight lines on the salt flats. Go do tai chi. Everything will work out. Trust me?"

"Bikram," he says. "I don't have the patience for tai chi anymore."

Inside, he turns on the chants and makes a smoothie, slowly peeling the oranges, removing pits from cherries with exquisite care. It isn't just Stan, he thinks, not just the Deserted, but all of them, playing roles they'd developed until they were trapped in those roles. Until they didn't even remember they *were* roles. After his wife's confession, the house was silent for days. She locked herself in her studio with her easels, while the producer sat by the pool and tried to find something to say. Everything he came up with sounded inadequate—too witty, too cruel, too dramatically effective. They were things the Deserted would say.

On a low rise half a mile from the Ancient Ruins, the nine sit around the fire in postures of resentment, disbelief, and terror. Shaneequio helps Candy wrap the ankle she sprained during the flight from the elephants. Bernatelli is silent and furious. Alejandra's eyes are dry.

"The thing about math," she says, in a black-and-white pickup interview, "is you can get it right, you know? I tell these kids all the time, stick with the procedures, don't take shortcuts, you get the right answer. What they don't get—what I'm trying to tell them— is that life isn't like that. You get out of school, everything's messed up. There aren't any formulas. You can't check your answers at the back of the book.

"Enjoy it while you can, I tell them. Every day. That's what I love about it. But you get out here"—cut to the Week One water polo match, a slo-mo shot of Stan nailing her with a coconut squarely between the shoulder blades—"let's just say it's not so clear. Let's just say people don't stick to the rules. There are no rules. When you get down to it, everyone's in it for themselves. That's just life."

"Maybe we should go north tomorrow, toward this ice field?" says Richard, leaning over a parchment map. The jungle is still, the birds silent.

"Why?" asks Bernatelli. "That where you left your Bette Midler records?"

Richard pouts. Shaneequio, spoon-feeding Simon, looks up. "Yo, what the fuck you think, you in charge here? You want to test that shit out?" Bernatelli takes a step before Clarice gets between them. Hiroko watches Candy. Alejandra does not cry. Night comes quickly, like a mugger throwing a sack over its victim's head. Tomorrow the Deserted will face the wrath of Xiolticanqatzl. This may be the darkest night of their lives.

Under the tarp, Gloria Hamm tries to sleep, mittens on her hands to keep from scratching. Simon's breathing is an excruciating rasp; the others listen, alone with their thoughts.

"You're gonna wonder what you did to deserve it, how you got from point A to point B," Alejandra says in voice-over. "Nobody's gonna help you then. Nobody's got time for you, all trying to take care of number one. So my advice to you is, enjoy it while you can."

When the universe was created, the only light came from the moon. They called this silver ball "Xim," the Sky Mother, and bathed in her radiance, and the people of the island lived happily together. But Xim could not do everything. She couldn't make the crops grow or show the hunters where to find prey. The people began to starve and fight each other. They prayed for Xim to help. Soon the ground rumbled and the volcano erupted in a blaze of color and the sun shot into the silvery sky.

They called him "Xiolticanqatzl," the Fire Father, the Vengeful One. Xim and Xiolticanqatzl fought a great battle, and then the Sky Mother and the Fire Father retreated to opposite sides of the firmament. The people built temples to please Xiolticanqatzl, where they stored their treasures: gold that shone like the Fire Father, gems that captured his light in stone, savory meals made of the goodness he brought forth from the earth. They punished criminals in the Fire Father's Isolation Chamber. But over the generations, the island people grew distant from Xiolticanqatzl. They prayed less and focused on hedonistic pleasures. In time, Xiolticanqatzl grew angry. The people stopped coming to the temples and eventually forgot where they'd built them, and all the island's riches were lost to the ages. And Xiolticanqatzl waited . . .

Until now.

"Pretty cool how they got that footage of the sun's actual birth," Paco says, panting. "Didn't know they had time-lapse photography back then."

"Actually, the sun was only born about forty years ago, didn't you know?" says Taylette. "It was during a Jimi Hendrix concert. That's why all the psychedelics."

"You spare some of that Powerade?" Taylette takes a long chug from her bottle, passes it to Paco on the next treadmill. The fitness center is crowded, most of the crew preferring to come at night when the heat has abated. Beyond the cardio machines, the benches clang with free weights; through an interior window can be seen eight pairs of legs scissoring in synch. "Who knew the kitchen girls looked so good in loincloths?" Paco says, nodding at the plasma screens. "Maybe El Lobo oughtta think about a midnight snack . . ."

"Do they get paid for extra work?" says Taylette, slowing to a sweaty walk. "They're Indonesian, does that mean they're below the line?"

"Right," says the producer.

"Too bad. If there was money, I'd jump on board," says Taylette.

"Shit you'd look fine in a loincloth, mamacita," Paco winks. "Totally got the back for it."

Taylette cocks her fingers, gun-style. "Right back atcha."

Last night's constellations sent the Deserted west, deep into the bush, a part of the island so thickly overgrown the advance team had to go in with chainsaws. They'd hiked through the night—Candy limping heavily on a walking stick carved by Shaneequio, Simon in a litter carried in shifts, Gloria trudging glumly at the rear—and arrived at the banks of the Canqaxim'po River just before dawn, the ruins of Xiolticanqatzl's temple crowning a hilltop on the other side. After a brief rest, they gathered at the riverbank, where they had to race through a thicket of hornet nests, steal a jar of honey set up on a stump, fish a key out of the goop with their tongues, and race back to unlock a mini-fridge that held breakfast. The winner of the race gained immunity from the Isolation Chamber; the loser had to ford the river's Class IV rapids and secure a zip line to the far bank.

"Shit, look at the maricón go!" Paco says, watching the edited sequence on the screens. The camerawork is flawless, the powerful water crashing just so. Richard's determination is engraved on his brow as he forces his way through the rapids with the kind of grit much beloved of Chevrolet and Tylenol ad execs. What the cameras don't show are the leeches clamping onto his legs, burying their eggs in his skin. They won't show those eggs hatching, the larvae burrowing into his flesh. "Makes the Marine look like a little pussy, don't he?"

"I always thought the Marine was a pussy," says Taylette. "I think he stuffs his shorts."

"Yeah? That true, Bossman?"

"Don't know, Lobo," the producer says. "Afraid of the competition?"

Normally the producer would never set foot in the fitness center, but the heater in his trailer still isn't working and Bikram without heat is like sex without friction. Plus, since the call with Boby, he's resolved to pay more attention to what his assistants are doing.

Perhaps he's been absent too long, locked away in his trailer while events take shape outside his control.

The AP hacks out a laugh, steps off the machine. "Call me Paco, man. And Bernatelli can have the lawyer chick, cool by me. That one's probably a dead fish in the sack."

"Don't let Kaminski hear that," says Taylette. "He picked her in the pool."

"Fuckin Kaminski. Remember that chick he took in Argentina? Only gymnast on earth who doesn't like it on top." He shakes his head in sorrow. "Sad-ass motherfucker."

"Some conference call, huh?" the producer says. He watches Paco with one eye while the Deserted, split into teams of three, roll giant boulders across the ruins. "You believe that asshole?"

Paco towels sweat out of his hair. "Coulda seen that shit coming, though, Bossman. All about the bottom line these days. No more winging it, right?" He steps off the treadmill and shades his eyes, staring into the Pilates room. "We got the Rockettes in here or something?"

"Well, don't worry," the producer says. "I'm not going to let him run the show. God knows what bullshit he'd come up with."

Paco watches the leg kicks, perhaps a second too long. "I'm not worried," he says. The Deserted have scattered through the ruins with blowguns, crouching into small, concealed spaces—all except Gloria Hamm, who strolls at the base of Xiolticanqatzl's pyramid, admiring the carvings of jackals, sea monsters, gods with triangular heads. When a dart misses her by inches, she trips and falls clumsily to her knees.

"Catch a steam?" Paco asks Taylette.

"Towel or no towel?"

"Ooh, baby, you're talking the language of Lobo," he says. "Look, Boss, Boby's gonna do what he's gonna do, right? Just because he's a bitch doesn't mean he's always wrong. Give him a chance. Maybe you'll like what he comes up with."

The producer grips the handles of the elliptical machine, watches his pulse climb on the display. "What if they'd come down on Animal Planet and said they wanted you to stage a war between the lions and the horses? What if they said they wanted to put all the sharks in tutus and teach them ballet?"

Paco stares at him. "They can do that?"

"I'm just saying—wouldn't that have felt, I don't know, like a betrayal?"

The AP whispers something to Taylette, who nods and heads toward the sauna. Paco, towel draped over his shoulders, leans against the next machine. "Who's betrayed, Boss? Some fat fuckin mechanic and his wife, chain smoking on their couch? A bunch of stoned teenagers feeling each other up? Bluehairs who haven't left their condo in years? You think someone's betraying them?" The producer's pulse rate has been replaced by blinking hyphens. "It's fuckin TV. It's a product. You can't make people buy a product they don't want. And if they don't want what you're selling, who are you to say that's their fault?"

"So we keep dumbing it down? Where's the bottom, Paco? Why don't we try to offer something smarter? If we treat them like adults, maybe they'll learn to want it."

Paco turns his head as though he hasn't heard right. "You're shitting me, right?"

"The more we show them this"—he gestures at the screen, where Shaneequio and Candy are flirting next to Xiolticanqatzl's well; cut to Bernatelli dipping a dart in poison—"the more this is what they want. We're supposed to be showing them *real life*, Paco. We're supposed to be showing them themselves. Isn't that our product?"

"Dude," he says. "This *is* themselves."

All around them, the whirr and squeak of cardio machines. From the back of the room comes a grunt and a roar as Hector bench-presses 295 pounds. Paco had taken it hard when Alejandra found the skull, earning herself a night in the isolation chamber. He'd turned away from the producer in mute fury, knowing there was no chance of an override.

The producer sighs. "Is Boby serious about this guest star thing?"

Paco ignores the question. "I'll tell you what would be smarter." He nods at the screen, where Gloria has taken cover beneath a blackberry thicket. "Maybe the dentist chick could talk once in a while, you know? Even something for the B-roll would help . . ."

"If she talks, she talks," the producer says. Boby's email this morning had been chummy, conspiratorial, a crude attempt to win the producer back to his side: *How about a country singer? Wld bump up our share w/the NASCAR demo. Mylee wld hate it, but I'll back u up—bros before hos, right?*

"Just saying," says Paco. Then, as if the idea were just dawning on him, "What if we get the others to turn against her? What if she does something to piss them off, or they *think* she did something? Maybe she'd wake up, get a little more involved . . ."

"You still want this show," the producer says. He stares straight ahead, past crew members on treadmills, on bikes, all of them unrecognizable from this perspective. The elliptical machine says, COOL DOWN. "Don't you?"

Paco stares at him a good long while, then throws a heavy arm over his shoulders. "Nah, Boss. I just want to make it with those kitchen girls. The show's all yours."

As Paco heads for the sauna, the producer watches Alejandra's face, frozen in fear as she's lowered into a deep well in Xiolticanqatzl's temple. This night will mark a turning point for the maudlin math teacher, a chance to confront her fears, forge her strength in the belly of the Fire Father, emerge in the first light of morning, transformed.

But there will be no transformation for Simon, only the long and painful trip home. Watch now as the sun sets in digital splendor behind eight silhouettes on the river bank, the players bidding farewell to another fallen comrade. As the theme starts to play, the credits zipping up the screen, watch them slowly lower Simon's body, wrapped in shrouds marked with the network logo, into the rushing Canqaxim'po, where he'll be buffeted by the current, swept down through the foothills, and caught by a medical team waiting at the takeout. His agent is beside herself—but we all know Simon could write poems for a thousand years and never make half of what he'll get for these three weeks on the island. He'd be lucky to make the per diem.

"'When I got fears that I might cease to be,'" says Shaneequio, hand over heart, as the body disappears in the froth, "'afore my pen has gleaned my teeming brain . . .'"

The credits unspool; the screen goes dark. Under the production company's graphic comes a woman's terrified cry: "Please let me out of here! Guys, please? Help—I don't want to be alone!"

It's long past midnight when he enters Control B, the backup module set a hundred yards behind the command center. He's momentarily disoriented by the stillness, the tomb-dark space broken by bright monitors, green and red meters, the low harmony of cooling fans. He's been unable to sleep for days—despite the image of Gloria on his monitors, he can't help thinking about Stan adrift on the network skiff, about Simon careening down the river in a body bag. By now they're probably getting lap dances in the Dubai Tower—but their misery had been all too real. It was their greatest fear, something equivalent to death: to be banished, written out, told that their lives, or whatever crazy version of their lives they'd chosen to tell, no longer fit in the storyline. For a few weeks, or a month, someone had wanted to tell a story about them. But then someone lost interest.

This was what they hadn't foreseen, what he and Armand had left out of the pitch: the desperation, the bottomless need for the camera's affirmation. This was what went unmentioned at the Emmys, at corporate retreats where the suits toasted them for dragging the network out of last place. Five seasons of celebration, of magazine covers, of standing ovations when he walked down Burbank hallways. Free will was a revelation—after decades of ever-more-manufactured entertainment, who would have guessed that the key to ratings was to let go of the reins, let reality take its natural shape?

Then Benin.

Now, in Control B, he slides into a chair and logs into the system with codes belonging to a fired tape logger. He rubs his arms against the artificial chill, punches up a live shot of Gloria Hamm, who tosses and turns at the edge of the shelter, muttering to herself and scratching fiercely. She has a wet shirt lain over her midriff, wet bandannas tied around her arms, but the itch is still excruciating, her pulse close to 100, her body tense as a guywire. As he watches, she sits up and puts her face in her hands, her eyes red-rimmed and teary. Everyone else is asleep. She's as alone as Alejandra, whimpering at the bottom of the isolation chamber, as alone as Stan Clewes floating on the endless sea.

Such a small thing, to alleviate this suffering, he thinks. The push of a button, to make someone happy. It's not intervention, though he doesn't know what to call it. Gloria's suffering is real—she isn't performing it or playing it up for the cameras, so how could it be wrong to quietly take it away? He'd brought her here, built this island-sized torture chamber. Wasn't it the least he could do?

He browses through the medical software, tags a few potential remedies: *sleep aids, topical antihistamines, herbicides.* Before he can send the commands, he's startled by a noise: the sequence of beeps and the heavy click of someone entering the control room. He kills the monitor, slides under the console just as the metal door yawns open. Heart pounding, the producer bites his lip, slows his breathing. Maybe it's Paco, he thinks, on a date with one of the kitchen girls; or a couple of techs finding a quiet place to cut some lines. He listens intently but hears only a chair squeaking, the tapping of keys, then the amplified sound of a telephone dialing. When a woman answers, her small voice filling the room, the producer slips out from under the console and moves on all fours toward the exit.

"I see you," the woman says. He freezes behind a humming stack of video servers. "Say hello," she says. Though he can't see her face, the intimacy in her voice stabs him somewhere near his solar plexus. "Can you say hello?"

The producer feels his hands sweating. He looks up into the shadows but can't find the spycam, presses his back to the equipment, scouts the fastest path out of the room. A second later, a strange sound comes from the speakers: an odd, throaty squeal, distorted by volume, unsettling. He holds his breath and peers around the servers. On a large test monitor, the improbable image of a baby stares out at Control B. It's a girl, with deep, dark eyes and a swirl of black hair; though her face is flattened by proximity to the camera, smeared by low resolution, he sees at a glance that there's something wrong with her. Her face is blank and strangely slack, her eyes dull and drowsy; she's being held by someone off-camera—her mother, probably—who takes her wrist and waves.

"Hello, my sweet little one. Hello there. Hello," someone inside the room says. The baby's mother jounces her; the baby's head lolls and she makes the screeching, gargling sound again. The producer crawls along the back wall, entranced. "Oh, beautiful little girl, Daddy misses you so much. Are you letting mother get some rest?"

Patel sits in a high-backed chair, profile lit blue and white. He's wearing a headset, leaning forward into the round eye of a webcam. "Oooga booga boo," he says. The child does not look into the camera. Something warm and unwelcome bells up in the producer's throat. "Oooga booga boo. Daddy loves yoooo. Oooga booga boo . . ."

When the child's mother comes on the monitor—round-faced and lightly freckled, not quite pretty, her hair pulled back accentuating the exhaustion in her face—the producer slowly backs toward the door.

"I think she seems better," says Patel's wife. "I can't be sure."

"What did the doctor say?" Patel says.

"He said the same thing as the last doctor. They all say the same thing: It's too early; things can quickly change; stay optimistic." She holds the unresisting baby to her shoulder. "How can I be optimistic if they don't tell me anything?"

"You need to sleep, *kanna*. Tell your mother to stay awake, so you can sleep."

"She's tired, too. She spends the whole day with the other children." The producer stops at the door and looks back. "We miss you, *nana*," says Patel's wife, her tired eyes searching for someone thousands of miles away.

"Four more weeks. Then I'm coming home."

"And then you'll leave again."

"Don't be so sure of that."

Gently, so gently, the producer eases the door open and crawls into humidity. When he's clear of the building, he lets out a gasp, leans on his knees, and stares into the dense jungle, at the looming backdrop of mountains, until the image of Patel's wife fades back into the darkness. Somewhere out there, the ancient cave sits silent and empty, waiting for his imagination to fill it.

No, he thinks, not empty. There's something in that cave, invisible but real. Something that can't be manipulated or cancelled. The trick is to find it, he thinks. To see it close up. Wasn't that what the show was about?

In another part of the island, Gloria is still sleepless, tormented by her own body and by her companions' indifference. She flails atop her sleeping bag, mutters curses, claws at her legs with enough force to draw blood.

What would she have thought, the producer wonders, if the agonizing itch had suddenly stopped? The wind drops, leaving a damp, expectant silence around him. If her suffering ended, would she understand what had happened? If she were granted a reprieve, would it occur to her that someone was watching out for her, or would she think it was some kind of trick?

After three weeks on this island, could she even imagine someone cared?

WEEK FOUR

■

. . . previously

The Deserted have lost their first two players—Stan, who was dragged off by jackals, and Simon, whose leg could not be saved by poetry or prayer. After a night in the isolation chamber, Alejandra returned to camp shaken, unable to eat the stew of manioc and tree bark Clarice made for the group. Candy might be making a switch from Bernatelli to Shaneequio, and Hiroko's waiting in the wings to pick up where the blonde bombshell leaves off. The only thing that kept the panic from overwhelming him, from crushing him like aluminum foil, the producer discovered, was to sit in a dark room and make noises to himself—open his mouth and let a string of meaningless syllables stream out one atop the other, something chanted and vaguely melodic, always straining to resolve into intelligible speech. He had the sense there was a word he was trying to say—a word he'd never heard, maybe a word that did not yet exist, and his lips and tongue were trying out every possible shape in order to find it. He had no idea what the word meant. Sometimes he'd mutter these sounds to himself in his car or walking down the street, to stave off the jittery, unreal feeling of an attack, to relieve some pressure in his chest; sometimes, forgetting himself, he'd start to babble in public, sitting at a coffeeshop or having a drink with a friend. One friend from the acting class he no longer took finally asked if he knew how strange it was. "It's inhuman," the friend told the producer. "It's like what I think hell would sound like." But the producer couldn't stop, he didn't want to stop, until he had discovered the secret word. It was out there, somewhere, waiting for him—like the strange presence that waits on the island, biding its time, something unexpected and terrifying that won't be satisfied until it comes face to face with the eight unsuspecting Deserted . . .

"Hey Rachel, great job with the quicksand!" he says. "Tyrell, my man, how about those Sixers?" The crew hustles straight-kneed through the sunny dining complex, scrolling their iPhones, Twittering, posting to the blogs under rotating pseudonyms. Bluetooth earpieces glow at their temples.

"Pei, we've got refrigeration issues for the luau. When's good for you?"

"Chris, I don't care what it costs to heat that lava—I want real steam, not CGI!"

"Still not working, Coco. Can you send someone over today? If I don't do some yoga, everyone in this Facility's going to regret it."

He's met with blank stares, burned-out expressions, all the symptoms of fourth-week slump. Stumbling through the glass-roofed corridors, under the sun dazzling through the canopy, the crew look like zombies in a greenhouse. When he speaks to them they grow wide-eyed, as though they've just received terrible news.

"Wassup, Bossman?" says Paco, when the producer sets his tray down. "Breaking bread with the little people?"

The producer ignores the jibe. "What's the latest?"

Paco considers a spare rib between his fingers, tilts his chin strategically, and gnaws the last bit of meat. He's unshaven, squinting from fatigue or glare or bong hits. His black T-shirt reads MATERIAL GIRL in silver letters. "Hiroko's out of pretzels. Richard's beefworm's getting beefy. Otherwise, nada mucho. More grab-ass with Candy and the gangbanger. Oh," he says, putting down the polished bone, "kinda weird: All the goats died."

"The goats?"

"In the livestock holding area. For the finale? This morning they're all stiff, legs all up in the air and shit."

The producer considers this as he stares into his curry. Across the dining room, a group of interns watches a replay of Shaneequio's Week Two hot-coal fiasco on a plasma screen. Someone has mashed it up with the Blue Öyster Cult song "Burnin' for You."

"Man, I hope that shit with Candy turns into a threesome. We haven't had a good DP since, like, Mongolia," says the AP. "Least, not among the Deserted."

"What about the dental hygienist?"

"Who?"

"Gloria," says the producer, but Paco knew exactly whom he meant.

"Nah. Doesn't seem like the threesome type."

It's been five days since Simon went down the river, and without him and Stan the dynamics are changing. Alejandra has been toughened by her night alone—once the hallucinations subsided, her crying jags gave way to stony determination, a nothing-left-to-lose attitude with a nasty streak. Since their make-out session, Hiroko and Clarice have barely been able to look each other in the eye. Bernatelli is working harder than ever to keep control, but with Candy's attention wandering, he's looking isolated; the producer has been waiting for Shaneequio to stab him in the eye, but so far no luck. Things are as uncertain as they've been since Week One, and no one can say who'll be next to go. Vegas has Shaneequio at 3-to-2, but the producer thinks that's wrong—and he's right.

Still, it's not enough for Boby. He's been pushing the guest star thing, his latest idea being basketball coach Phil Jackson. "He's the Zen Master!" Boby said. "Be like some guru shit, like *Apocalypse Now*, dig? 'The horror! The horror!'" His latest fax was a photocopy of his ass, with a crude bumblebee drawn in and the caption *Your BEE-hind is on the line.*

"The good news," says Paco, "is Alejandra solved the new star map. They should hit the labyrinth tomorrow." He nods at the plasma screen, the looped slo-mo shot of Shaneequio pitching hands-first into the coals. "Sure he's looking forward to it."

"A little bird tells me *ET* is holding six minutes for him on Thursday. You know anything about that? Someone leaking?"

The AP shrugs and pushes his tray away. On the table next to him sits *Loving God with All Your Mind*, tiny colored flags sticking out from dozens of marked pages. "Not me, jefe. I got my money on your dentist lady," he says. "Feel like her luck's about to run out."

The producer studies him a moment, as a shadow sweeps from one end of the dining complex to the other. Through the glass dome he can see black clouds racing, just the latest unscheduled climate event, what he's come to think of as "Weather Gone Wild."

"Let me ask you something, Lobo," he says, picking at his plate with chopsticks.

Paco balls his napkin, hits an eight-footer into a trash can. "Paco."

"What if there was no show?"

Paco rubs his temples. "Man, you gotta lighten up. Boby just likes to sound important. Remember when he was Cathy Harmon's little bitch? I never seen you get so uptight—"

"I don't mean cancellation. I mean if there was no show. If this was all . . . real."

Paco hands his tray to one of the service staff and belches deeply. "You mean if there was just, like, *randomly* ten people who survived a midair explosion and found the keys to new SUVs in coconuts? You mean if wild horses just naturally grew saddles? And Coldplay decided, like, for no reason, to do a show on a deserted island?" The kitchen staff is clearing the lunch buffet, young girls lifting steel trays with oven mitts bearing the network logo. Paco laughs. "There's always a show, Bossman. Only difference is who's putting it on. Don't get too deep in your own head, you know?"

"But if you met these people on the street or a hiking trail, and they acted this way, would you believe it? Would any of it seem remotely real?"

Paco steeples his hands under his chin and appears to take this very seriously. Behind him, Miley comes in from the fitness center, flushed and damp in a tank top and running shorts.

"Thing is, B, believing or not believing—it doesn't really figure in. Who knows if the Deserted even believe themselves? Or maybe they do. Fuck, I don't know. It's like, this shit transcends belief."

"But why? Why can't we make a show people would believe?"

The AP meets his gaze and holds it. "Because it would be boring."

"So people would rather be lied to than bored? They'd rather have their intelligence insulted?"

"Wouldn't you?"

Miley strolls past the empty steam trays and snatches a banana from a fruit cart. "Hi, boys," she says, cocking a hip next to the table. "Want to watch me eat this?"

"I'll watch you eat *this*, mamacita," Paco says.

"Catfights, gay baiting, winner take all . . . Isn't *this* boring?" he says. Yesterday, the Deserted plunged their bare arms into a giant termite mound; the player who withstood it the longest won a week back home with the spouse of another player. After the Volcanic Labyrinth, the rundown reads *Monkey Urine Drinking Contest.* "Isn't there room for something new?"

In Antarctica, they'd wrestled in a tank of seal blubber. In Nicaragua, they'd held a boa constrictor kissing contest—maybe at the exact moment his wife's car was flying into the ravine.

"Life isn't new, Boss," Paco says. "It's the same shit over and over. Just gotta go with it. Like this book says, long as you try to force the world to do what you want, it'll frustrate the shit out of you. I found this on an airplane. Like someone left it for me, see what I'm saying?" He holds the book out, jiggles it sardonically. "Wanna borrow it?"

"Was there another catfight?" Miley says.

"I just don't know how long we can keep topping ourselves," the producer says. "What are we supposed to do next, human sacrifice? A nuclear detonation?" His voice has gotten louder, the interns at the next table stealing glances. "We can't do this forever."

Paco sets the book down, laces his hands behind his head. "I don't think forever's something we gotta worry about."

It took the L.A. county sheriff's office close to a week to get through, and when they did the producer couldn't understand what they were saying. "We can't use it," he kept telling the deputy. "We can't use it. We don't do cops." When they finally sent his wife's dental records to Nicaragua via diplomatic pouch, they were accompanied by a small, sealed bag that he weighed in his palm without experiencing anything he would call emotion. The ring was blackened, fine scratches of gold visible underneath the char. He imagined it as still feeling hot. The fact that she'd been wearing it was frank and significant, but that significance would not clarify itself in his mind, dispersing instead into the air around him like water splashing away from a stone.

"Look, you want to go over the dailies with me? I have to deal with the beefworm at four," Miley says. Then, glancing at Paco: "Don't even bother."

The larvae Richard picked up in the Canqaxim'po have begun lancing into his flesh, traveling inexorably upward. By the end of the week, they'll start disrupting his nervous system, clouding his cerebrospinal fluid. "He's starting to sound a little loopy," Miley says. "This morning Shaneequio found him talking to a tree."

"Maybe it was his fairy godmother," says Paco.

The plasma screen now shows a clip of two women arguing over chores. "I'm sick of your [bleep], you little bitch," one says. "You think everyone here is supposed to serve you, like you're the [bleep] queen or something!" For a moment, the producer can't recognize them. His head swims from lack of sleep, the pent-up energy of days without yoga. He fingers the stone in his pocket. After a few seconds, he realizes the clip isn't from the island—the players are from several seasons ago. Grand Teton, maybe. Or Mongolia. Was one of these women the DP?

"It's time," Miley says later. They're sitting on a picnic bench, backs to the Facility. Over the nearby ocean, glare battles with gloom, cloud shadows clashing and pulling apart on the water's surface.

"Are those our clouds?" he says.

"Did you hear me?"

"No." He peers at his laptop editor, scrolls through termite-mound footage, browses for suitable music. Something country, he thinks. Tammy Wynette?

Miley sets her laptop on the bench and stretches her legs. The air is moist, a nervous wind breathing up from the south. The producer can faintly smell her sweat and a waft of strawberry body spray. "We can't afford her anymore," she says carefully. "Not with so much riding on this season. She does something or she's gone. Lobo and I agree."

"One of a Kind" ought to work, he thinks. The rights will cost a fortune, but let Boby deal with that. Maybe his peeps at Endeavor can help. He drags the song into audio under an image of Gloria Hamm, shoulder-deep in the mound. As the strings swell, she obligingly looks off into the distance. Her mouth is crusted with sunburn or dried food; he has an urge to gently rub it off with his thumb.

"Is this a coup?" he asks Miley.

"Don't go there, okay? I'm trying to watch your back. Do you not give a shit anymore?" On the day his wife left, he'd sat by the pool watching hummingbirds strafe the bougainvillea along the stone wall. They hovered nervously, then darted into the distance, and their flight felt attuned to his thoughts; in the daze of sunshine and mojitos, her voice was dreamlike, inconsequential. The hummingbirds returned, the buzz of their wings subliminal, and he felt as though he were controlling their movements. With a thought, he could send them off into oblivion; with another, he could bring them swiftly back.

"She's nobody," Miley is saying. "She's not attractive, she's not funny, she barely talks. She hasn't screwed anyone, no one hates her, no one complains about her. She's wallpaper. *I* have more text-votes than she does.

"Look at this," she says, then snatches away his machine and logs into the social network software they started using two seasons ago. She punches up the global matrix view, and the Deserted's nodes light up on the monitor, the complex web of interactions and moods between them represented by glowing threads. "Look at these values: Bernatelli is hot with absolutely everybody. Richard, same thing. Candy and Shaneequio are cooler but with more variance in their contact colors. Do you see it?" she says. "There's nothing complicated here—these links mean votes. Viewer mail, blog posts, calls to the network, news coverage—whatever metric you want to use—"

"I don't care."

"Oh?" She hits a button and the screen changes, the relational data switching to individual view. Gloria Hamm shows up as a small blue dot, blinking against an empty black field. "Do you care about this?"

The producer watches the blinking light for a long moment. When he looks up at Miley, her hair damp and sticking to her temples, there's the scar again: pink and cruel, marring otherwise magazine-ready features.

"We have to be smart now," she says. "Every player has to be useful. To give us something. We're three weeks away—it's time to start thinking endgame."

He turns back to Gloria, blinking in her sea of black. "People don't have to be useful."

"They do on television!"

He closes his eyes, summons a long, cleansing Ujayyi breath. Far out over the ocean, there's a low roll of unauthorized thunder. If he had a social network analysis of his crew, he might know what Miley's really up to, whose back she's really watching. With each day the feeling of being out of the loop grows stronger, the sense of invisible cabals whispering out of earshot. *Her luck's about to run out*, Paco had said. But it isn't about luck: not when the click of a mouse determines what you get to eat or whether you sleep, not when the storyboards map out your narrative's rise and fall. And its end. He watches Gloria's dot blinking, and a line from Armand's favorite poem comes to him: *All times I have enjoyed greatly, have suffered greatly, both with those that loved me, and alone.* He thinks again of the skiff, sees himself floating out on that dark sea. *The long day wanes; the slow moon climbs . . .*

"How did you get your scar?" he asks Miley. She straightens; her face goes through a series of expressions: surprise, confusion, embarrassment. "Did someone cut you?" He hadn't known this was what he suspected until now. "Someone cut you, didn't they?"

She stands abruptly, her voice rising half an octave. "What's happening to you?" When she arrived in Benin, she'd soothed all of them with her unflappability, her efficient cool in the face of trauma. But now her hands are shaking, her face flushed: it's a terrific performance, with all the hallmarks of real rage. "Do you give a shit about anyone on this crew, everyone who busts their ass for you?" She flings an arm toward the Facility, all angles and glares in the jungle behind them. "You think they care about Gloria Hamm? They're doing their jobs. Jobs you hired them to do."

"And who hired you?" he says.

Her mouth opens; her shoulders sag in dismay. She sits, runs a hand through her hair. "Look, I know it's been a bad year. It's been rough for you. We all get that—"

"Don't," he says.

"No one would fault you for stepping back, you know? No one outside this Facility even needs to know. Take some time, relax. God knows you've earned it."

"You'd like that?" he mutters. He lifts his eyes to hers. "You and Lobo."

Miley purses her lips. "You know what? Fuck you." She punches up a shot of Bernatelli standing on a rise, considering the ocean by starlight. "Look at it," she says. "*This* is a player." Bernatelli is shirtless, his muscled back to the camera; the producer thinks he looks like an ad for a gay dating network. "Don't turn this into you-against-the-world. You think Boby's going to stick with you? When you started this show he was in the *eighth grade*!"

She leans over his editor, scrolls to the beginning of Gloria's termite footage, deletes the sequence with a savage click. The producer puts his hand over hers.

"Miley," he says.

But she snatches her hand from his grasp. "If you want to fuck someone, try Personnel." She logs out, whisks her laptop off the bench. His screen is blank except for the networking package, one tiny blue dot blinking in space.

Ten yards away, Miley stops, her back to him, and looks up into the thick branches. A spycam gets seven seconds of her trying to regain her self-control. "Just kidding," she says, eyes closed. He can barely hear her over the sputtering wind. "Catch you at sponsor call?"

He listens to her footsteps recede up the trail. Turning back to his editor, he hits a few keys, undoes her deletion, leans back to watch Gloria take a nap. He chooses a Beethoven sonata, drops it into audio, sends the whole file to his private server. Maybe this is the clip that will help him sleep.

For a while he watches Gloria's blue node flashing, thinks of her out there, in the heart of the island, tries to imagine where he himself is located in the void that surrounds her. He closes his eyes, imagines tendrils sprouting from that blue dot, spreading across monitors and mainframes and into the buzzing ether in search of his own blinking light.

When he opens his eyes, the screen looks the same. Maybe the dot is a little smaller. Using his administrator password, he resets the data so the Deserted are once again equal: blank slates, equally alone. You can't just write someone off, he thinks. Just because they don't excite you, because they're no longer useful—you don't just put them on the skiff and walk away.

But the social networking analysis is backed up. Every ninety minutes the program saves its data set, transmits it to Burbank, runs reports keyed for rate of change, quality of relations, predicted trajectory, comparisons with previous seasons, matched against various vectors of audience response. A PowerPoint presentation generates each Friday. On the island, only the producer and his assistants have access. He thinks they have a monopoly on information. He's wrong.

"People think I'm hard. They think I'm a hard guy. They look at me—my face, the way I talk, my abs—I can't blame them. Maybe I am hard. I'm a hard worker. A hard fighter. I play hard, think hard, [bleep] hard—" Bernatelli laughs boyishly, turns to someone off-camera. "Can I say that? But you know, I might be hard on the outside, but I'm a person, too. I've got feelings. Things get to me, just like anyone else. But am I gonna show that to you? Am I gonna throw the game away, put myself or my soldiers in danger?" He points a finger, stares icily into the lens. "Not a chance, bud. Not Walter Bernatelli."

He did two tours in Iraq, saw more combat than you'd care to know. He earned a Bronze Star in Fallujah for carrying five wounded Marines across a heavily mined highway. He would have gone back for a third tour, but he was called home to care for a sick family member. All this and more is included in his casting file, along with headshot, screen test, psych-eval, and action photos: shirtless, with rifle.

"Here's what you learn in the desert: Feelings kill. You think the terrorists care how you feel? You think they're gonna sit down for a heart-to-heart? So you can feel all you want to—I got all the sympathy in the world. But when his men need him, Walter Bernatelli gets the job done. You want a therapist? Want to cry on someone's shoulder? Better find another sergeant."

"So I tell him, dude, I gotta clip this mike somewhere, right?" says an audio tech. "You don't put on a shirt, you're not gonna be too psyched where I clip it to!" He dribbles, fakes past Hector, pulls up, and shoots a clanger off the rim. Paco grabs the rebound and works his way around the key while Patel tries to swat the ball away.

"Homeboy don't need no microphone," Hector says, nodding at the nearby plasma screen. The basketball court swelters in the midday sun, a small crowd of accountants watching from the back door of the fitness center. "Homeboy lets actions speak for themselves, feel?"

"Man, other day we're trying to do like a kickboxing thing?" Paco says. "And here's the gangbanger, talking to Alejandra about *logic*. Some shit about Descartes." He passes behind his back to Hector. "I'm all, *that's* not going on the air."

"We playing ball or telling stories?" the producer says.

"That's a walk!" says another tech.

"Fuck you," Hector shouts, then elevates for a powerful dunk.

"No basket," says the tech. "It's a fucking walk."

Hector takes a step. "You sure about that, bitch?"

"Alright, let's just calm down," the producer says. But the chief engineer is already chest-to-chest with the two techs. Paco and Patel wrestle at mid-court for the ball. "I said calm the fuck down, people! Can we play some fucking hoops? Dammit!"

All five stop to look at the producer, whose arms are flung wide in frustration. Paco sputters into laughter. "Think fast, Boss," he says, pretending to fling the ball at the producer's head. The producer flinches.

"That's game, anyways," says Hector, now engaging in a complex handshake with the tech who'd confronted him. Paco turns and hurls a jumpshot, which goes far wide of the basket and bounces off into the trees.

"Go get that," he tells the audio tech.

"Blow me."

"Go get that and I'll give you the code for the girls' trailer." The tech sprints after the ball. "What'd you think?" Paco asks the producer. On the plasma screen Bernatelli, Hiroko, Clarice, and Richard are struggling through the Volcanic Labyrinth, shouting to be heard over the roar of lava. The close-up of Bernatelli is masterful, capturing the ruddy roughness of his skin, cut of his jaw, trickles of sweat beading through his five-o'clock shadow. "Some camera work, right?"

"Right."

"Didn't even need the fixed cams," Paco says. "Good thing we got those cover shots in Pre, though."

"You never leave a man behind," the ex-Marine says in voice-over, while in the labyrinth he half-drags a swooning Richard away from a deadly jet of steam. They'd had to bring in new camera operators from Seoul, the Americans refusing to enter the labyrinth without hazard pay. There had been unpleasant discussions with the union. The union now finds itself under federal investigation. "I don't care if it's your worst enemy," Bernatelli says. "You don't leave him behind. You stay until the job's done."

"Pretty cool how it went down, too," Paco says. "Like some *Saving Private Ryan* shit."

Hector, towel around his neck, puts an arm on Paco's shoulder. He's a full head taller than the AP, his face almost perfectly square. "Oh Walter, you saved my life," he says in falsetto. "I love you, Walter, can I fuck your tight, white ass?"

"Looks like the dentist's got some game after all, huh, Boss?" Paco says. "Too bad about Candy, though. Guess Bernatelli and Shaneequio gotta find something else to fight over."

"Like Descartes," says Hector, and the two men crack up.

The producer takes Patel's elbow. "You have time to talk about that thing?" He nods toward the bench.

"Thing?"

"That I asked you about."

"Maybe they'll fight over Gloria," says a tech. Hector and Paco double over.

"I think we should talk about it later," Patel says under his breath.

"How about a segment where she brushes their teeth?" says the tech who brought the ball back. "Or maybe she's got a drill, like in that movie—you know: 'Is it safe?'"

Paco swats the ball away, sets, and hits a three-pointer. "How about you leave the storyline to the professionals. Stick to wiring, like a good little geek."

The Deserted had split into two teams, the first to get through the labyrinth winning Carnival cruises, four bars of soap, and a map of the Treacherous Ice Flats. Bernatelli's team lagged from the start, slowed by Richard's gibbering fear of molten rock. When the hairdresser collapsed a mile from the finish line, Bernatelli doubled back and carried him the rest of the way, just as he'd carried his comrades in Fallujah. In the command center they'd watched in awe. Taylette declared her intention to "make a baby with that beautiful American."

The other team, led by a newly ruthless Alejandra, opened an early lead, but midway through the labyrinth tragedy struck: Gloria's shoelaces caught fire, and kneeling to blow them out, she stumbled backward, knocking Candy off the path. Shaneequio, with a heroic dive, caught the corporate lawyer's hair in his fist, but even his strength could not hold, and the player voted "Most Babe-a-licious" by readers of *Maxim* plunged, shrieking, into the burning river of lava.

"Well?" he says to Patel, while Hector and Paco practice alley-oops.

"I don't like it at all."

"The cave? You're telling me we can't use it?"

"The secrecy," he says, barely moving his lips. "Why can't you tell the APs? I don't understand what you need. The APs can assign techs and equipment; they can talk to the network—"

"No network," he coughs. He turns Patel away from the court. "Listen: *I* don't know what I need. I just want a general sense. Is it usable, or not?"

"Why don't we build a sound stage, shoot some exteriors, then use chroma-key for the actual scene? It would be much simpler that way. Less of an insurance risk, too."

A droning sound rises through the trees: a network plane glides low overhead, pontoons gleaming. The bar will be freshly stocked tonight, the PX jammed with toiletries, new DVDs, condoms. Someone from HR will leave a packet of mail outside the producer's trailer, all the envelopes carefully steamed open and resealed.

He leans closer to Patel. "I don't want to fake this."

The techs have drawn Hector and Paco into a game of half-court, two-on-two. The techs are getting killed. "Dude, is it true we got Paris Hilton?" says Hector, dribbling between his legs. "You hook me up with some face time?"

The audio tech leans on his knees, panting. "You want her *face*?"

Paco takes the pass, hits a quick layup. "Lo siento, man." He sounds truly sorry. "Boby ran it up the flagpole. Suits said they want someone more aggressive, to like sharpen the brand or something."

"More aggressive?" Hector says. "Fuck do they want, some serial killer?"

"Two words," says the other tech. "Jenna fucking Jameson."

Patel slumps on the bench. His complexion is dark, his upper lip pale where he recently shaved his mustache. It gives him a child-like air, as though he'd daubed himself with paint. "Yes, we can do something," he tells the producer. "Two cameras. Lighting will be tricky. Audio won't be pleased. And I don't know where we would set up a signal relay. But you'll say I can't talk to Hector."

"Not yet."

"We'll have to send a crew to clean it. There is so much guano and slime—"

"We'll use it exactly how it is. Otherwise there's no point."

One of the techs comes limping off the court. "Sub in?" Paco calls. The producer ignores him. Someone on the court says, "Pussy."

The pressure has been building, tingling in his extremities during meditation, squeezing his lungs when he tries to sleep. On the Facility's shaded paths he's struck by dread, by the urge to shelter in a tight space. In the shower, he finds himself huddling in the corner, water spattering on his head. He'd thought a game of hoops would help. He'd thought to hurl himself into the fray, throw a few elbows, run hard, sweat out the fire. But it isn't enough. There's no release on the island—he suspects he couldn't even vomit properly, that the necessary muscles would lock up and refuse to do it.

"Have you had time to read what I sent you?" Patel asks. The producer has a vague recollection of email attachments, PDFs, various and sundry links. The word "arsenic" swims faintly in his mind. "It could make a great project."

"Sure you're right about that. Let's talk in a week or so."

"I hope to put a pitch together directly after the finale. If you're on board, studios will be more receptive."

"On board?"

"You two want another game, or what?" Paco calls out. "We only got fifteen minutes—Hector here's got a date."

One tech lets out a wolf whistle. The other says, "Who's Miley's best boy?"

"You'll think about it?" Patel says.

"Who's in for Hold 'Em tonight?" says Hector. "Fridge'll be stocked. They even got some of that nasty-ass Indian whiskey for you, Patel. Let's get Lobo fucked up and take all his money."

"In your dreams, flaco. Besides, Patel's got a date in Control B, right stud?"

One of the techs says, "We're playing 'I Never' at eleven, boys' trailer."

"Here's one," says Hector. "I never seen such a fuckwit AP." He dances out of range of Paco's kick.

"I never titty-fucked Rachel from Enviro," says the tech.

"Drink!" says the other.

Paco stands next to the producer, bouncing the ball without looking at him. "Hands off the medical server tonight, Patel," he says. Patel is startled, looks from Paco to the producer and back. "Don't even be thinking about intervening, homeboy. I know you got the hots for the Chinese chick."

Patel is scandalized. "That is not true! I didn't touch the medical server!"

"No? Somebody was in there. Somebody I guess didn't get the memo." Without looking, he flips the ball to a sprinting Hector, who breaks for the basket and does a two-handed slam dunk, hanging on the rim and kicking wildly. "Bossman says no intervention, that means no intervention. Even if your favorite player's in trouble. What was the Benadryl for, she get like stung by a bee or something?"

"I thought that chick was Japanese," Hector calls, still hanging on the rim.

Patel folds his arms in indignation. The pale spot where his mustache had been quivers visibly. Paco gives him a slow grin, then punches him on the arm. "Chill, man. I know it wasn't you."

"I never had a date with a tranny," says one of the techs.

"I never jacked off to a picture of my biology professor," says the other.

With studied casualness, Paco turns to the producer. "How about you, Boss?"

The producer reaches into his pocket for the stone. "How about what?"

"You coming tonight? You'd be good at this game, all that shit you never do."

For a moment no one speaks. The techs stare, confused as third graders at a physics conference. When the basketball rolls to his feet, the producer flips it into the air with one sneaker, catches it, and places it firmly into Paco's breadbasket.

"I never drink, Lobo," he says, and heads for the fitness center.

On the plasma screen, the seven remaining players have collapsed outside the labyrinth, shielding their eyes from the blinding sun. Gloria huddles apart from the others, incredulous, staring back into the volcanic glow.

As he enters the shade of the building, Paco calls after him: "First time for everything, B."

He has to admit, it's a pretty good teaser: the lone, robed figure sitting in pale starlight atop a gleaming, snow-covered knoll. The world is dark, the mountains sinister, the only sound the fateful panting of the sled dogs who wait at the figure's side. It's a cruel world, full of dangers only partly glimpsed. Down below, a flicker emerges from the forest: seven ant-like shadows start the laborious trek across the ice flats.

They've survived explosions, volcanoes, ancient gods, and each other's lies . . .

The light moves slowly over the tundra. As the seven shadows spread across the icy plain, the sled dogs start to bay. From beneath the robe a graceful, feminine hand reaches out to pet the animals: her familiars. She turns in partial profile, only a tantalizing glimpse of rimless glasses and full lips visible under her hood.

But can they survive . . . her?

"Suitably macabre. Your idea?" says Armand.

"Not exactly." The producer is on hands and knees, a spelunker's light strapped to his forehead, trying to decipher the wiring of his trailer's heating system. His fingers are covered in grease. The inside of the mechanism looks as if a bag of colored yarn exploded.

"Call it 'strategic capitulation.' It costs me less to run with this crap than to get into it with Boby."

"Choose your battles."

"Something like that. Plus, you'd be surprised how cheap she was." Spying what might be a loose connection deep inside the wall, the producer slides a hand between wires and receives a distinct shock that spreads ice up to his neck. "Motherfucker," he says, stomping across the hardwood. He snatches the light from his head and flings it across the room, then cringes as it narrowly misses the glass doors of his rock display.

"Well, she's a great get," Armand says. "A little tacky, but you'll see your share go up ten, twelve points."

"He's going to milk it for every dime he can, then cancel us. Why should I break my back to stop him? Let him think I'm toeing the line. I've got bigger fish."

"Your cave," Armand says. "I can't say I understand what you're after. Not that I don't have total faith in your vision, of course . . ."

The producer stands in mountain pose and forces his jaw to relax, his breathing to slow. Last night Alejandra woke from a terrible dream: It was the Sky Mother, the goddess Xim, who showed her a frightful vision. "She's angry at our trespasses. She demands reparations," Alejandra said. She sat shivering beneath the stars for hours, squinting at the arcane patterns. Toward dawn she used Shane-equio's knife to hack off most of her hair. Seizing Bernatelli's map, she drew a lipstick X on the spot where Xim's priestess awaited.

"Ever think about the old days?" the producer says.

Armand laughs and lights a cigarette. "Constantly. Did you know that the martini glasses in my office were self-chilling? Who's ever heard of such a thing?"

The producer sweeps his arms overhead, swoops down and flattens his palms on the hardwood. "I've been thinking about *The Wrecking Ball*."

Armand blows out smoke. "Of course you have. You wouldn't be an artist if you didn't romanticize your own obscurity."

"It's not that," he says, his hamstrings aflame, lower back threatening to spasm. "It was just so simple. We showed up, we made someone happy." Slowly he sinks to his knees in child's pose. "It wasn't about getting a leg up on anybody, or revenge. There was no backstabbing, no secret crack habits, no cheating spouses . . ."

"Is that what this is about?" Armand says.

The producer presses his cheek to the cool floor. "No."

The houses were always a mess: sagging eaves, rotted siding, masonry like stale cornflakes. Sometimes a car up on blocks in the yard, or a rusted swingset. By the end of a week, the roof was off, a new floor plan starting to take shape. At the end of the season, what you had was something solid—glitzy or modest, sprawling or compact, it didn't matter, the owners always got weak-kneed in a way you couldn't fake. And in the end you had a new home: you walked through spacious rooms, smelled the paint, touched the counters. No one could deny those houses. No one wondered if they'd disappear the minute you turned your back.

"I just don't recognize these people," he says. "I don't know what they are." Kneeling, he clasps his hands on the hardwood and bows his head, leans forward, lets his legs float up into a headstand. "Was it always like this? Back in the Everglades—were they all screwing each other all the time?"

"I remember one young woman—a masseuse, if I recall? From Providence, was it?—who seemed to be screwing *you* all the time," Armand says.

"It's 'massage technician.' And you did okay, too," he says. "Remember the Maghreb?"

"The Golden Age," Armand sighs. "Those Arab men. I felt just like Peter O'Toole."

"All I'm saying is, it used to mean something. Paco says it doesn't matter anymore if it's real or not. But it does. It does matter. Doesn't it?" The producer's legs sway overhead; his stone falls from his pocket and lands on the floor with a sharp crack. "In a million years you wouldn't think to do the things they do. But it's not random. They all do the same things. It's almost like there's a script. But who's writing it?"

"Televolution," Armand says. "Isn't that what Miley calls it?"

"It's more than that." Slowly, he lowers his legs until his toes touch the floor. "It's inhuman."

Armand lights another cigarette. "What's inhuman is what you're doing to that poor hairdresser. Really—have you noticed his lisp getting worse?"

"That's the thing. We're not doing it. He is."

"Well, make him stop. He'll never get the Marine if he keeps acting so faggy."

With an exhale, the producer lets his hips roll forward, flattens against the floor. "I don't know why I call you," he groans.

On snowshoes and cross-country skis, the Deserted make their way across the ice flats. Clarice powers past Shaneequio, throwing a sneaky elbow into his gut; Richard stabs his pole at Bernatelli's shoes. Alejandra, her short hair giving her a fierce aspect, takes Hiroko by the shoulders and throws her into a snowdrift. Cut to the gleaming hillside, the rising moon, baying dogs, the sinister presence watching their advance.

"Can anyone hate each other this much?" he mutters.

"Who is it that thinks you can approach the High Priestess of Xim?" says the robed figure, standing with her dogs as the Deserted struggle with crampons and ice axes.

Bernatelli drops to one knee and crosses himself. "Seven humble travelers."

"Pretty darn humble," the priestess says, looking down at them, her voice bright and bubbling with mockery. "What exactly am I supposed ta do for ya?"

"High Priestess," says Bernatelli, "we come to ask your wisdom and guidance on our path to Paradise."

"What's in it for the priestess?" she says. "Nothing comes for free, ya know."

"We have no worldly goods to offer you. Only our gratitude, our obedience, and one systems analyst—" A cry from the back of the group as Shaneequio, Alejandra, and Hiroko shove Clarice forward, where she falls to the snow at the priestess's feet. "She's a hard worker, and loyal. She will serve you well."

The priestess considers. "What you're about to hear," Armand says, "is the sound of thirty-five million viewers squealing in delight."

"That's kinda more like it," the priestess says, pulling back her hood with a wink and a dazzling smile. "The goddess will see you now."

But there are no houses anymore, the producer thinks as they go to commercial. No blueprints. Nothing tangible. Personalities, hopes, motivations, private terrors—everything is negotiable, subordinate to the needs not just of his show, but of the Show, the vast ethereal river of manufactured drama and garish infantile emotion that stretches overhead like its own too-bright heaven. You used to have to knock two or three times, until the quiet, abashed art teacher opened the door a crack so you could tell her that life was about to change; but now they throw themselves at you like a pack of dogs at a meat truck. They would do anything, say anything—or no, not anything, only what was dramatically effective. What was useful. As though they'd been waiting their whole lives to be made part of the Show, to be given the chance to serve it. And once they got that chance, every crude, nasty, selfish urge they'd ever had came blazing out, stoked and validated by the Show's unspoken needs.

"Welcome to Xim's Temple," says Sarah Palin. "What took you people so long?"

"Armand, the other night," he says. "I did something—"

"Wait just one second," Armand says.

In the ice hut, the Deserted are arrayed at the high priestess's feet. Clarice, in a novice's robes, circulates with a tray of steaming teacups. Torchlight gleams off pristine walls, the broad ice altar strung with prayer flags, flanked by marble statues of Xim.

"For centuries I've waited here," says the priestess, "so I can give you some wisdom and so you can understand about Xim and all the terrific things about her and just pay your respect."

The Deserted bow their heads, muttering their respect for Xim.

Maybe that's what it amounts to, he thinks. A new religion. A set of sacred narratives they've agreed to believe in, however absurd, degrading, patently ludicrous those narratives may be. The more ludicrous the better. Not script: scripture. And like any religion, its first commandment is belief—active, unquestioning belief—because even one person's disbelief threatens everyone else's right to believe, threatens the very possibility of belief, and is, therefore, the worst possible sin, punishable by death—or death's equivalent: exclusion, exile, erasure.

But how could anyone still believe? Where once you had wood and steel and concrete, now you had termite mounds built in the scene shop. You had monkey piss, air-guitar contests, votes cast with human finger bones. After Benin you had an endless litany of obstacles and ordeals, of corporate-sponsored luxury and comic-book deprivation and Soviet-style confessions. What had once been about free will, about the unpredictable ways of the heart, all of it had been overridden by the Show with its one, paramount directive: Crush everything in your path. How was *this* related to reality? Where were the real tragedies, the breath-stealing disappointments? Where were the heart attacks, the sudden headaches, the tumors? Where were the vicious husbands? The failed and embarrassing attempts at sex? The dark hours of self-loathing? The devastating insults let loose before kindness thought better? Where were the fathers who worked their whole lives only to collapse, unseen, in cheap motel rooms? Where were the wives who soared off the road? In all this bravado, where was the total failure of hope?

"Armand, I think someone might have seen me—"

"Shhh!"

The priestess sits on her dais of ice, Shaneequio's head in her lap. "You can't spend your life crying over spilt milk," she says. "Being a whiner. What's already happened is the past, and only if people aren't interested in progressing themselves, people who just like to kind of complain and whine and put other people in charge to sit there worrying."

"Candy . . ." Shaneequio sobs.

"Candy was a nice girl, but the question now is, are you going to sit here and complain or do what made this country a great place and kinda pick yourself up by those bootstraps and succeed!" She strokes Shaneequio's hair. "You have to forget all those negative memories. That's not what winners do."

"I was trying to help," the producer says. "Is that so wrong?"

But who was he trying to help? Since the day on the basketball court, he's felt sure Paco is planning something. He can't say why—a slight hesitation when he gives an intern an errand, anonymous changes to the rundown, edits that seem to undo themselves. But the AP can't be working alone—Hector must be in on it, maybe Patel, or even Boby. In theory, it's impossible—the software should log any calls to the network, should BCC him any unauthorized emails. But in theory, all the goats should still be alive. In theory, there shouldn't be a red tide off Paradise Beach. Theories have been breaking down recently, and the producer can no longer afford to let events be shaped by other hands.

"Now your problem," Sarah tells Alejandra, "is that thinking like a teacher! Have you ever seen a teacher really succeed at anything? Are there any teacher war heroes you can think about? Teacher astronauts? Teacher presidents? How do you help with winning yourself if you're always so busy trying to teach lots of things they aren't needing there."

Alejandra bows, accepting the priestess's wisdom. One by one, Sarah speaks to the Deserted, coaches them to put aside their fears, their heartaches, their friendships. "Are you here to get the Nobel Prize for being nice, or for winning?"

"Armand, are you listening to me?"

"What's that? Yes, of course—oh wait, just a second," he says, "I have another call. I think it's Liz."

On the live camera, five of the Deserted creep up on Richard, sleeping on the floor of the ice hut. One by one, they pummel him with pillowcases filled with bars of soap. The hairdresser cries out pitifully. But on the island, no one can hear you scream.

"Now what I see here is seven people who maybe just think they're a little too smart for the rest of us, who think, you know, some fancy diploma is going to help them when you really get down to the nitty-gritty of being all you can and winning everything that you want to be." The priestess stands above the prostrate Deserted, in a shimmering gown of gold and silver thread. "But being smart and thinking you're so smart is not the thing that made this country great," she says. "So the thing making this country the amazing, perfect place, people who don't know the meaning of 'quit' and who fight and are so strong they won't ever stop doing what they want just because some negative person with some fancy diploma says it's different. So the question is, which ones of you are that people and the ones that are quitters and who's a winner?"

The Deserted groan and writhe like penitents in a charismatic church. On the floor of his trailer, the producer clutches his stone, his back starting to cramp.

"It takes sacrifice. The kind I'm talking about which says, 'It's not always all about me.' The sacrifice, that when everything works in the spirit of the founders. And it just feels so darn good, just sacrificing. That's what makes America such a gosh-darn great place where business is business, and you know that someone isn't as good as you. So you have to kind of change your thinking and realize that what made the dream was what our fathers up there were founding for us, and sacrificing. You can't think all the time about 'me, me, me,' or this idea of what that person is, that secular humanism that's not found with faith. It's not about the me you know: It's about *you*—the you you have to be when you're progressing that dream.

"Who is that me that I'm always kinda thinking about? Where are *you*? In America! So you can be any me that you want to be better. That's right. When someone tells you you can't, well, that's not the real America! No one has the right to be better than you, you're gonna take charge and be that person winning. Not 'me,' not Walter the Marine, or Allie the teacher, or, like, Shinquom the criminal type of person. The truth that we were founding there with God and faith is that it's up to us individuals, and we aren't the only ones. Not for one gosh-darn second!

"So if you're not me, who are you?" Sarah says, beaming at their dense, eager faces. "You're the person who's *playing* you. It's so darned simple! You're playing that person, that you. And what for? For that movie, that great big terrific movie. About you. Not 'me'—you're the star in a movie about that me's life. You! And gosh darnit if you don't want it to be just the best movie anyone's ever seen. Full of interesting stuff, and conflict, and struggle, everything that makes us great like the best people.

"Now, in Hollywood, those people who just love money so

much, who aren't founded in America, they make a different kind of movie, with people always doing 'me' things. But the movie I'm talking about, it says we really are that shining country on a hill that we found. Full of conviction and not quitting that made us so terrific, like God wants. That's the kind of movie you win, and if they get in your way they know how strong you are and you'll have faith and win and your movie is the best one that everyone wants to see that it's your God-given right.

"You don't *ever* say quit, and you don't *ever* die. If someone tries to be a better movie you aren't weak—you're gonna show them you're stronger. You don't let anyone take your movie, and if that python spirit says evildoing near it you're gonna grab that sucker and step on the back of its neck and break it, you break that spirit, and crack its skull and crush its brain until it begs and the spirit is gone. If you love your movie, you'll break that python. Would you let someone take your beautiful baby or crack the python first and rip out its spine? That's what I mean! You crack it! Did Benjamin Franklin let them take his movie away, and we wouldn't be here today. A line in the sand and a cherry tree—they made the country like the founders, and you're going to draw your own revolution and win for that movie you love because it's God's right as a winner. That's what the Sky Mother wants. There's just no stopping all the ways you can progress to be stronger, and when your movie is the best, you're the one that's winning."

She raises her arms in benediction. "Amen."

The Deserted bow their heads. "Amen."

The producer closes his eyes and says a mantra.

In Burbank, a jeroboam of champagne is seething on Boby's desk.

"Are you still there?" the producer says, rolling onto his side and hugging his knees. "Armand?"

In the silence he feels again the slow advance of a silky hand of dread. "What if there were no show?" he'd asked Paco—but maybe, in any real sense, there isn't, not anymore. If everything is the Show, then nothing is, and if there's no show, then there's no need for a producer—he might as well vanish, pack up his trailer in the middle of the night, and leave the story. Somewhere they're fueling a skiff with his name on it.

The Deserted don parkas and snowshoes and head back to the tundra. All but Gloria Hamm, who still kneels before the priestess as though waiting to ask her something. Since Candy's fall, Gloria has seemed more engaged, even energized. The others speak to her more often; they assign her tasks with a certain deference. The priestess, smiling wickedly, stoops to whisper in her ear.

"Armand?" says the producer, shivering on the hardwood. The windows are jeweled with darkness, as though a velvet curtain has fallen upon the trailer.

As the credits roll up the screen, Gloria's face remains—faint, like an afterimage, glowing as though touched by inspiration.

"Armand, where the hell did you go?"

WEEK FIVE

■

Once, there were ten. They were tough. They were cunning, cou-
rageous, determined to brave the island's dangers and be the first
to get to Paradise. But the island had other plans. Jackals. Electrical storms. Termites. Volcanoes. And the terrifying vengeance
of the Sky Mother. Now it comes down to six—hungry, filthy,
but unbowed, each one bent on victory at any cost. Alejandra has
emerged as a leader to rival Bernatelli, who lost his Candy first to
Shaneequio, then to the island's wrath. Back home his younger
brother, who has long struggled with bipolar disorder, has started
electroconvulsive therapy, desperate for any relief. Hiroko, once so
canny in her flirtations, is growing weak from malnutrition, while
her husband of three years spends every night in Milwaukee's Asian
transvestite clubs. The others have grown cautious around Gloria,
the sleeper, who shrewdly sent Candy plunging to her demise. By
the time the producer was hired as the host of *The Wrecking Ball*,
the panic attacks were safely in the past. It was in the second season
that they rebuilt a house in the San Jacinto mountains east of L.A.,

a tottering old A-frame owned by a young painter. Though she was duly grateful, she regarded the whole proceeding—and the producer—with wry bemusement, her laughter dry but gusting suddenly and unexpectedly lovely, like that of a startled bird. Over the weeks the producer found himself playing to that laughter, provoking it, showing her the brushed steel fixtures, the French window casings, the remodeled studio with its majestic view, pointing all these out with the exaggerated flourish of a carnival barker, wanting only to sweep her up in the enthusiasm the whole crew worked to project. A month after the finale, she sent him a canvas, an impressionist painting of the new house, the autumnal blaze of the surrounding woods, two blurred and unidentifiable faces in an upstairs window. They corresponded for almost a year and were married toward the end of his last season on *The Wrecking Ball*. Armand was the best man. Unexpectedly happy, the producer sometimes sat with her by the pool of their new home, watching the sunset, and the faint echo of that strange, secret word would occur to him, the slightly embarrassing but distant thought of the days when he'd spilled those dark, inscrutable sounds. He had never discovered it, never found the mysterious combination of syllables, and yet if he closed his eyes he knew it was inside him, safely embedded in the warm, wet tissue around his heart. But there's no rest for the wicked—and already the ill winds of the Mangrove Swamp are drifting across the island in search of the unsuspecting Deserted. There are storms brewing in the mountains, even bigger storms brewing between the players, and no one on either side of the camera is expecting the magnitude 8.1 earthquake about to strike two hundred miles southeast of the island, nor the towering wave of destruction it's bound to create. They'd better hold their breath, and brush up on their breaststroke—it's Week Five and no one knows what the island will throw at them next. Find out now.

The red phone rings at a quarter to four in the morning, waking him from an anxious dream of sharks, gaping jaws rushing through black water. "Can you come to the command center?" Patel says. His voice is low and taut, as though someone were holding a gun to his head.

"Why are you calling me?"

There's a shrill, sobbing noise in the background. "Come to the command center."

"There are policies, Patel. Is it an act of God?" But the phone has gone dead.

Trudging through the rainforest in flip-flops and shorts, behind a fading flashlight beam, he rehearses the many ways he could fire the director, testing each line for maximum cruelty. Patel's email barrage of spreadsheets, environmental reports, and old photos of gaping pits in the earth has started to strain his patience; when the director isn't clogging his server, it seems, he's locked in Control B Skyping with his wife. Last season he'd been a model team member, absolutely dependable, but this time around Patel's focus may be slipping. Yesterday they had to reshoot the entire camel race because of lousy fixed-cam angles; the day before, a pre-dawn encounter between Alejandra and Bernatelli, which may or may not have amounted to sexual assault, went untaped. When you add these screw-ups to the dead goats, freak hailstorm, etc., can anyone doubt the producer is in the crosshairs?

"Time to get a clue, Daddy-O," Boby said in conference. "Time for freestylin' is, like, way over." The plastic speaker vibrated as though it contained a swarm of insects. "You don't make some decisions, Homes, someone's going to make it for you, dig?"

It's as though the Palin triumph—the days of hysterical blog posts, talk radio, the clips of "Sarah's Sermon" circulating endlessly on the Internet—never happened. The pressure from Burbank is relentless, hotter than ever; all the more reason to finally figure out what to do with the cave. All the more reason to keep his own focus.

He'd called Armand late last night, desperate for a few laughs, for stories about the good old days. But the phone just rang and rang.

The jungle is muggy, the ground damp. When the flashlight dims and winks out, the producer is left in a breathing darkness full of shivers and crackles. A familiar tingle climbs the back of his neck, a creeping sense of disembodiment. Off balance, he leans against the broad trunk of a mahogany tree, listens to the pulse in his ears. An owl hoots high up in the weave—it sounds like a real owl, but it's hard to be sure. Insect sounds flare and recede; the wind shakes spatters of rain from the canopy. The ocean swells, crashes, draws back with a throaty rattle. How much of this is enhanced, he has no idea, and the confusion only sharpens his vertigo. The darkness rises to towering proportions, a wet weight that presses down and around him. He touches his face, his chest, bites his thumb to assure himself he still *has* a body, flattens his face to the bark.

Ujayyi breath, he thinks, forcing his mind to slow. He closes his eyes, tries to envision the island from above, to see the whole of it, its shape and contours. He tries to project himself through the jungle—to the windswept moors, the ice flats, the sculpted dunes. Somewhere, the Deserted are breathing in this same darkness. He holds onto this thought, tries to push back the fear with it—they are here, flesh and blood; if he is thinking of them, maybe the Deserted can sense him, too. He imagines Gloria Hamm staring into the night, wondering who, or what, might be out there, imagines her blue light blinking faster, a bright silver line snaking toward him, connecting her to him.

The image brings some dimension to the darkness, a geometry that tames it. A coyote howls in the near distance, and he struggles to his feet, T-shirt damp with sweat. Fucking Paco. He makes a mental note to delete the coyote at the first opportunity.

In the command center, a hushed tension presides. Patel leans forward in the producer's chair, hands laced behind his head. Techs stand around in silence. Paco, who looks as though he has not yet slept, nervously taps his front teeth with a fingernail. A voice blasts from the speakers, wild and wretched.

"*God! It hurts! Where are you? Please! Oh, god help me, it hurts!*"

"Someone turn that down?" the producer shouts, but no one moves.

"*Oh, god, god . . . how dare you! Please! Oh, please, help me! They're coming!*"

"Ninety minutes of this," Paco says.

On the main screen, lit in night-vision gray, Richard lurches around the desert camp—now on all fours, now reeling wildly, hurling himself at the tent where the other five huddle. He's naked except for a pair of loose, filthy briefs, the muscles of his arms and legs rope-taut and spasming.

"Whose idea was this?" the producer says.

"*Listen, please—listen to me!*" He clutches at Hiroko's leg; the postal worker, clad in a jade kimono, tries to hide behind Bernatelli and Alejandra. "*You have to listen!*" he says. "*You have to—*" A shock of pain twists his torso, knocks him onto his back. Behind him, dunes rise smooth and undulate in crystal moonlight, under a density of constellations, stars that shoot according to a randomizer.

Richard springs up and grabs Gloria by the shoulders. "*Are you listening?*" he says. His eyes roll back and he unleashes an incoherent cry. Everyone in the control room covers their ears. "*We're in danger,*" Richard says, shaking Gloria until Bernatelli pulls him away. He lunges at the Marine, barking in his face in a series of high-pitched yips.

"Someone want to tell me what the fuck's going on?" the producer says, evicting Patel from the chair with a glance.

Paco, swaying noticeably, says, "Beefworm, nervous system," then belches and drops into a swivel chair.

"He's been awake all night," Patel says. "Talking about the 'spirits of the island.' He says the spirits are trying to kill all of them."

A tech at the medical console says, "A hundred and four!"

"What spirits?" says the producer. Heaving for breath, Richard collapses into the sand, arches his back, and shrieks again. "For the love of Christ, Audio, turn it the fuck down."

Paco spins around and around in the chair, face turned to the ceiling. "Maybe Stan Clewes is back. Maybe that's what the little maricon's so scared of."

"Maybe he came back for a haircut!" says a tech. Two runners laugh obligingly.

"That shit ain't funny," says Paco.

"When Richard, he all screamin' an shit, he go, like, runnin' aroun' and shit and be all fallin' down, talkin' bout spirits and like some booshit, I's like, that mufucka got it *bad*, you feel?" Shaneequio, in an on-camera pickup, screws up his face in a cockeyed grimace. Over the weeks his speech has gone from clear and measured to nearly incomprehensible; they've started running subtitles to stress the point. "I's all, mufucka you got some *prollems*, yo. Like, fuck, and shit, you feel?"

Cut to Richard, on all fours, howling at the moon.

"Where's Miley?" the producer says. No one knows. They've called, texted, no response.

"Hector," says Audio.

"An I's thinkin', shit, if this mufucka gon die or some otha shit like that, who all's thinkin' bout Shaneequio, feel? Man's got ta look out fo hisself, y'know, like that crazy priestess tole it. I's thinkin', yo, mufucka, you got ta make sho he don be goin' *no*wheres. Cause if he go, you be goin' nex, an thas some col'har'd shit you got ta be watchin' out fo!"

"Yo, yo!" says Camera Two. "Like, mufuckin Shaneequio be in da *house*!"

"Shut your white ass," mutters Paco.

"He's a liability. We have to keep the unit strong," Bernatelli says to the others. They stand a few yards from the hairdresser, ready to flee if he attacks again. Only Gloria regards Richard with concern. "He'll just slow us down. We wait for him to pass out, then head for the swamp. We'll leave food and water."

"No way, yo," Shaneequio says.

"Are you some kind of fuckin' doctor?" Alejandra says, snapping her fingers and flouncing her head side to side. "What are you, like some medical *expert?*"

"We can do nothing for help him," Hiroko says. "He sick no matter what!"

"No one's more upset about this than me," Bernatelli says, laying an arm on Gloria's shoulders. "But we have to keep going. Someone will come for him."

"Who, mufucka?" Shaneequio says.

Richard rolls onto his side, stretches a pitiful arm toward the others. *"We have to get out of here,"* he moans. *"They're coming!"*

"One oh four point two," says the tech at the medical console.

Patel crouches by the producer's chair. "I think we need to do something," he says quietly. "This is getting dangerous."

"No."

"We're talking about a medical emergency—"

"No."

"Oh, Simon," Richard cries. *"Simon! Help me . . ."*

"Oh, Simon!" cries the chyron master. "Read me a poem, lover!"

"Splinter group's not a bad idea," says Paco. "If the dentist and the banger stay behind, we could follow them separately, get the two groups going against each other, like some *Lord of the Flies* shit. Worked in Patagonia."

"Forget it."

Out of the corner of his eye, the producer watches Paco and Patel. There's something in how they avoid each other's eyes, how they aren't interrupting each other, that's got all his red lights flashing.

"I be thinkin', like, Bernatelli he got Hiroko, mos def," says Shaneequio, "an like Alejandra an shit, she ain't gon make a move now cause he be stronger'n her so she got to wait, do somen mo sneaky an shit. So that leave me an Richard, an that otha lady, an if somen happen ta Richard, you know, it's like—boom!—like Shaneequio be fucked an shit!" He makes a series of intricate hand signs, flinging them at the camera. "Somebody got ta win this here shit, thas jus a fack. An I's thinkin', why not Shaneequio, feel?"

With a strangled gasp, Richard's body goes rigid, then starts to quiver and shake against the sand.

"Seizure!" cries the tech, with a note of triumph.

Patel says, "I really think—"

But the producer shoots out a hand and squeezes the director's arm.

From Richard's mouth comes a series of grunting, gulping breaths, followed by a rising bolus of foam. His head jerks painfully to one side, again and again. Cut to Steadicam, the better to capture his quivering Adam's apple, the twitches in his neck muscles and arms.

Hiroko, kimono falling open, hides her face in Bernatelli's armpit. Shaneequio and Alejandra just stare. Gloria, gaping at the others, sits and cradles Richard's head.

"See, that's what I'm talking about," Paco says. "Peas in a freakin pod."

"If you won't listen to me, at least think about the underwriters," Patel says. "They're going to ask why nobody intervened—"

"Be quiet," the producer says. The camera zooms in on Gloria, who smoothes Richard's hair, humming a tune too softly for the mics to pick up.

"We dedicate a field team," says Paco, "set aside like four minutes each week to check in with them two, some shit like that. Maybe six minutes. What do you think, Bossman? Might be enough to shut Boby up."

Patel consults with the tech at the medical console, then turns squarely to the producer's chair. "We cannot stand by while someone needs our help. I don't think that's what this show is about. Already we have one broken arm—"

"This show," the producer says, massaging his temples, "is about what I say it's about."

"This man is in trouble," says Patel, with unaccustomed vehemence. "If you won't—"

"What are we doing here?" the producer says, louder than he'd thought to. Then, suddenly, he's standing up, vaguely wishing he weren't. "Of course he's in trouble—is this reality? In reality people get into trouble. They get sick. They get hurt. People have to take care of them. It's messy. It's one big goddamned mess. Something fucking funny back there?" At the back of the room, two terrified interns shake their heads. "People get sick. They get diseases. They have accidents. That's how real life is. They drop dead. Is that news? Do you live in some kind of fantasy world? There are no happy endings!"

"Boss," says Paco.

"We don't do fantasy, so get that straight," he tells the director. "Whatever happens happens. We are not intervening. Period."

"Boss!"

"What?" He looks up just in time to see Richard lurch into the tent, snatch a hunting knife, and plunge it into his thigh.

"*Get out! Get out!*" Richard screams, twisting the blade as the others rush to stop him. Shaneequio catches a fist across the chin, but soon he and Bernatelli have immobilized the howling hair-dresser's arms. Alejandra sits atop his ankles. Hiroko is last seen running toward the dunes, kimono flapping. Two story assistants clutch each other by the fax machines. A twenty-year-old intern from Newhouse starts to hyperventilate.

"Puta madre," says Paco.

"Lobo," barks the producer. "Zip it."

Gloria kneels at Richard's side, pressing a towel to his soaked brow. The knife protrudes from his leg, sunk in two inches, blood oozing in time with his pulse.

"*Will you follow me?*" he says, his eyes fevered. His voice has become strange, raspy and hollow, as though someone added reverb to his channel.

"Audio?" says the producer.

"Not me," Audio says.

"*Follow me,*" Richard says.

"Yo, where you be talkin' 'bout follow you?" Shaneequio says.

"*To the Promised Land.*"

Paco moves closer to Patel, who leans an ear in his direction.

"Either one of you says another word, you're fired," the producer says. He knows now what's happening. It's all becoming clear: This is the chance his assistants have been waiting for.

"Time to make a choice, Boss," Paco says quietly. "Week Five, six players . . . someone's gotta go . . ."

"*Let me take you,*" Richard says, imploring the others. Alejandra squares her jaw, angrily blinks back tears. "*Don't leave me. Let me show you.*"

"I have to concur," says Patel, avoiding the producer's eyes. Even Gloria, kneeling wide-eyed next to Richard, seems to sense a sword about to fall. Somehow, while he wasn't looking, Paco and Patel have engineered this crisis; though nothing is supposed to happen outside his knowledge, somehow the trap has been sprung. If they sideline Gloria, he thinks, it's over; his control of the show, grown shakier with each passing day, will be broken.

"Where the hell is Miley?" the producer says, dropping into the chair. If Miley were here, he'd know what to do. He could fend off the mutiny. Then a terrible thought: That's exactly why she's not here.

Before he can fully absorb that, something extraordinary happens: Richard, knife still stuck in his leg, rolls up to all fours and starts drawing on the tent floor with his own blood.

"What the hell?" says Bernatelli.

Patel talks into his headset. "Suzy, can you get closer?"

Everyone leans forward to see what he's drawing—everyone but the producer, who somehow already knows. *"They're coming,"* Richard whispers, as the field team zooms in on the map of the island, drawn in great detail, almost perfectly to scale.

"One of you pussies tell them about the meteor crater?" Paco says, staring pointedly at Camera One.

"Fuck off, Lobo," he says. "Yeah," says the chyron master. "Suck my dick."

The producer reaches for his stone. How *could* Richard know about the crater? How could he know the location of the swamp, or the Wall of Doom? He watches with queasy déjà vu as Richard pulls the knife from his leg and drives it into the canvas.

"They're coming," he gasps.

"Who?" says Alejandra. "Who's coming?"

"The Deserted."

Bernatelli rolls his eyes and smirks. "That's us, bright boy."

"No," Richard says, and passes out in Gloria's arms.

As the shot comes in tight, the producer finds himself standing again, his body prickling with exultation and fear. The knife, gleaming with Richard's blood, marks a place they couldn't possibly know about, that none of the Deserted has ever seen, that hasn't even been coded into the stars. The producer pages Miley again, 911.

"I's all, what the fuck you talkin' bout, the Deserted ain't us? It ain't us, then who it be, yo? Thas some strange-ass shit, alls I can say." Shaneequio's voice closes the sequence, a shot of five players kneeling in a circle, hands joined in prayer, a startled Gloria back in the fold, saved for the moment by this unexpected development. Then back to the knife, which points to the exact location of the producer's cave.

"An this booshit bout some Promise Lan? I's tellin' you: Be some strange-ass shit goin' down on this island. Thas the mufuckin truth."

After two yogaless weeks, the heater is fixed. The producer sets aside late morning for a no-holds-barred, joint-blasting session of Bikram. All through story conference he's imagining it: the stretch and strain of tendons, the invigorating heat of Ujayyi breath, the tingling bliss of shavasana. He turns off all the monitors, sets his stone on the nightstand, a stupid smile taking over his face; he's barely through his first sun salutation when the red phone rings again.

"Act. Of. God!" he shouts into the receiver.

The earthquake struck far from land, twelve miles below the ocean. The tsunami it generated has already demolished miles of coastal villages in Irian Jaya and is heading straight for the island. The first thing that occurs to the producer is that Boby will probably blame this on him; the next is that Boby is probably responsible.

"Christ," he says. "Can we get the players to move to high ground? How far are they from the mountains?"

Colson "Coco" McPhee, facility manager, says, "It's not the players we need to worry about."

Turns out, there are a handful of bunkers under the Facility, built by Ballard Corp. shortly after the Cuban Missile Crisis. Once known only to certain members of the Facility and HR teams, the bunkers have become a haven for many a randy tech or their sexiled trailer-mates. When he descends the iron ladder nearest his quarters, the producer sinks into the overpowering smell of stale beer. The floor is littered with cigarette butts, energy bar wrappers, a used condom streaked with the print of a sneaker tread, glowing grotesquely in the purple light.

As soon as he pulls the cover shut, a clammy nervousness starts creeping up his legs. The bunker is no bigger than his bedroom, with a locker full of canned goods, a dead transistor radio, and a bulky, closed-circuit television which proves to have no audio; clips from seasons past—Patagonia, Grand Teton, Mongolia—run in a silent loop. In the far corner, a toilet with no seat. He considers resuming the Bikram—the heat he generates could warm the dank bunker almost to the comfortable point. But when he imagines the tsunami, imagines the Facility covered in acres of frothing water—the massive weight of it, just yards over his head—all he can do is sit on the edge of the musty, ancient cot and rock himself.

In the days since Richard's seizure, the Deserted have made little progress. Slowed by the burden of the hairdresser's litter, they'd had to sharply curtail the tango contest; the rescheduled monkey urine event had gone smoothly enough, but with Week Five slipping by the decision was made first to float the hang glider race, then cancel it entirely. Gloria's litter-hoisting stamina has earned her a temporary reprieve. Hiroko, however, has not stopped hiccuping since the scene at the desert camp; she wears the kimono night and day, its sash mysteriously loosening whenever Bernatelli is nearby. This morning before dawn, they came one by one to Richard's bedside to ask forgiveness for having beaten him with soap. The hairdresser, shivering and aphasic, touched a bloody fingertip to each of their eyelids.

"I'm sure you know what you're doing, big guy," Boby said. As the finale approaches, the senior VP has adopted a strategy of false cheer. "To an untrained eye, it might look aimless—but you're the genius. I wouldn't dream of interfering with your artistic vision. Rock on, brother!"

The Palin bump has cratered, the blogs are moribund, text votes at lower levels than anytime since the Steppe. It's what Armand used to call "rabbit time," as in: You'd better have one hell of a deep hat.

Hands trembling, the producer opens a tin of tuna, fiddles with the old TV: the Deserted fleeing a Teton avalanche, tiny figures racing below a swell of furious earth. Shadows menace the edges of his vision. A minute later, the bunker's iron cover opens with a squeal, and a pair of bare feet descends—polished toenails, a silver ring on the middle-right toe, a tanned set of silk-smooth calves.

"Go ahead and look up my dress," Miley says. "Like I give a Bedouin shit."

The producer leans back on the cot and tries not to show his relief. "I thought you might be the hit squad," he says. "That would make for one hell of a finale. Very meta."

Miley stares around the bunker, then turns off the TV. "We gotta talk." He makes room for her on the cot, but she crosses her arms—covering the tits, a bad sign—and says, "Where the fuck is my field team director?"

The producer scoops tuna with his index finger. "Pardon?"

"I've got five players out there ready to kill each other, another one at death's door. The Chinese mail lady looks like she's about to dig herself a hole—"

"She's Japanese."

"—and that's if the others don't drop her headfirst into the meteor crater. Not to mention we don't even have assignments for Week Seven, which by the way Boby's threatening to go *live* with, and now Suzy disappears with two cameramen and my best A2. So you're going to tell me," she says, then snatches the tuna tin from his hand and dashes it into the corner, "what in fuck's name is going on."

They stare at each other, until a twitch at the corner of her mouth gives her away.

"Nicely done," he says.

"You like that? It felt good. I got all Lara Croft on your ass."

"More like Joan Crawford."

"Who?"

"Never mind," he says, patting the greasy mattress.

She makes a gagging sound. "You expect me to touch that? With my body?" She sits on the bottom rung of the iron ladder. "Seriously—what the fuck?"

The producer studies his junior AP—her bright dress with the network logo, her hair pulled back in a ponytail. In the purple light, the scar at her jaw glows a faint, sickly green. The TV is dark, as if the avalanche swallowed the Deserted once and for all.

"You ever think about what happens to them?" he says. "I mean, after?"

"Recording contracts, books, eventually infomercials and bankruptcy court. Not my brief, really. I guess some of them go on other shows. I guess they're considered celebrities now, as if they've really done something."

"In the old days, if you were expelled from the tribe you were dead. You got eaten, or a rock fell on you. I don't know. Or you starved. Maybe you just sat down in the forest and waited."

"What was that, Season Three? Glad I wasn't around; it sounds dull."

"Think about it: It's not just death. Death, everyone knows about. Everyone's seen it: parents, siblings. But it's more than that. It's everything. It's the tribe. They're the whole world, the whole species. You don't know if there are others. There's your people and then there's everything else. And one day they say, 'We don't want you. You aren't one of us.' Then you're cast out, sent away into the forest . . ." The image of the skiff blinks into his mind, the silent bobbing of waves. "Well," he says, fighting a catch in his throat. "Can you imagine that kind of loneliness?"

From somewhere above comes a tortured, metallic groan. Both of them look up at the bunker cover, hidden in purple shadow.

"Meanwhile, we sit here and watch them drink monkey piss."

Miley nudges the squashed condom with the tip of her toe. "It's not real monkey piss."

Paco hadn't trusted her at first. He and Jonesie, her predecessor, had their own rhythms, their own jokes. Paco naturally saw Miley as a threat, thought circumstances had given her a leg up before half the crew even knew her name. He went out of his way to undermine her, to reverse her decisions, put down her ideas; all through Greenland they locked horns, but by the start of Season Eight they'd found a way to work together. When the producer asked Paco about it, the senior AP clammed up; finally Miley told him that she'd taken Paco out in the off-season, plied him with tequila, then bought him a lap-dance at a high-end gentleman's club and gone out to the parking lot and slashed his tires—a warning, she'd said, that he could work with her or against her. The producer has often repeated that story admiringly, though it occurs to him now that there are worse things than flat tires.

"What's the Promised Land?" she says.

He looks at her steadily. "I'm not ready to go into that."

"You're not—" she stops, gaping. "Sorry, what week is this?"

"Look, I'm still working some things out. Suzy will be back tomorrow. Your A2, too." Fuming, Miley paces the bunker, turns on the TV to footage of the Teton Vole-Chili Cookoff. Picks up a cigarette pack from a shelf, crumples it in her fist when it turns out to be empty. "It's not personal," he says. "I'm trying to do what's best for the show."

"Oh? When did that start?"

"If we're going down, I want it to be great. I want it to mean something. You want the last show to be some idiotic iguana-wrestling competition? See who can make the sexiest loincloth out of nutria fur? Is that how you want to be remembered? I tried to tell you, a few weeks ago. But now . . . I think I'll get it all set first. I'm sorry," he says. "I just can't take the risk."

Miley turns back slowly, with a show of dignity. Struggling to keep her face neutral, she sits on the ladder's bottom rung. "What do you think of Boby?" she says. "You think he's a nice guy? You know, fun to be around, all that?"

"What?"

"You think he's good-looking? You like that cologne he wears, Eau de Douchebag or something?" When he doesn't answer, she bites her lower lip and looks at the floor. "I bet you'd say he's hung like a pig in a blanket, wouldn't you? Men always think other men they don't like have tiny cocks. What if I told you Boby's pretty well hung?"

"Miley—"

"You ever imagine what it would be like to suck him off?" Now Miley's voice quavers. "I don't mean metaphorically. I mean you've got that little Saudi prick's cock sliding around in your mouth. You think you'd like that? While he's got Eminem on his office stereo, some kind of fucking *lava lamp* glowing on a table?"

He stares at the junior AP, at the cruel scar running along her jawline. Someone had betrayed her, he's sure of it now—a lover? a father?—someone she'd trusted enough to get that close. And he'd ruined her.

She raises her gaze, eyes dry and fierce. "Did you think we got this season for free?"

The producer shifts uncomfortably, cot springs jangling beneath his weight. "I never asked—"

"Yes you did! You asked all of us—and we all gave it to you. And for what? This . . . *vision*? Even you don't know what you mean anymore. No intervention? Do you think poker tables fall from the sky? Jesus, there are messages in the *stars*!"

"There's a difference," he says. But even as he says it, he knows he doesn't believe it. Miley's stare is intense; her hands are shaking. "There's still something worthwhile, something worth protecting. I can't explain it."

She stares a moment longer. "Do you know how old he is?" she says, then puts her face in her hands and sobs. His first instinct is to comfort her, but he's frozen by uncertainty—is this outburst genuine, or just another performance? He reaches into his pocket, but his stone is back at the trailer. On the TV, two players from Season Nine are Sumo wrestling, stripped down to boxer shorts, stalking each other in a circle of ice.

"I believed in you," Miley says. She blows her nose on the hem of her dress and stares discomfitingly at the producer. After her first miscarriage, his wife developed the habit of watching him for hours, barely blinking. She wasn't angry, she said, wasn't really thinking about anything; it was only that she couldn't take her eyes off him. "I think I need to know you're still here," she'd said. He tried to ignore it, but he couldn't read, couldn't watch TV, without squirming under her gaze. Pleading, he told her it made him feel as though he'd done something terribly wrong. With great effort, she pulled her eyes away. "You must have a guilty conscience," she said.

To Miley, the producer whispers, "Why?"

Another series of rumbles and creaks around the bunker. How many dead in Irian Jaya, he wonders? How much water, smashing heedless against the island? He thinks again of the cave, its pit of darkness the natives' only shelter against terrors from the sky, from the ocean, the jungle. They'd have had no idea why they were so unlucky, what they'd done to displease those unfathomable gods. What else could they do but draw pictures on the wall? It would have been the only way they knew to control it.

"Because I remember what the show used to be," Miley says. "I remember the first season. I was in grad school. My professors wanted you brought up on charges." They'd given the Deserted a week's worth of food and water, a tarpaulin, and two fanboats, then let them make their way through the Everglades. They'd had no idea what would happen.

"They were real people then," he says.

On the TV, a med student from Buffalo throws another player's clothes over a cliff, followed by a speeded-up montage of the players trying, and failing, to mount Mongolian donkeys.

"They were whores," Miley says bitterly. "All of them. But it didn't matter. It still doesn't. What matters is what you decide to do with what you have."

There's an abrupt, tinny beeping, and she glances at her Black-Berry, raises one eyebrow. "We could be here a while." She eyes the musty mattress, then comes to sit on the other side of the cot, pulling the dress tight around her legs. "Don't get any ideas."

For a time they sit side by side, leaning against cold concrete. The TV flickers silent and monochrome, the picture occasionally shrinking to a bright line and expanding again. Opening week in Mongolia: ten strangers brought together by a train derailment. Footage from Patagonia: three of the Deserted on a reward trip to a fancy restaurant in Puerto Montt. The table is crowded with tapas, fresh bread, and wine, the candlelight adding to the warmth in the players' eyes, an all-too-rare moment of camaraderie, before they headed back to burn each others' sleeping bags.

He doesn't feel himself drifting off until another beep from the BlackBerry startles him. "Maybe that's the all-clear?" he says. Drowsily, Miley shakes her head.

She gets up, stretches, walks to the ancient, rusty toilet. "Turn around," she says, and he does. Over the spattering, she says, "Anyway, the nutria loincloth thing's an idea. I can talk to Livestock—though after what happened with the goats I can't make any promises."

"It's a cave," he says. "The one I told you about."

She crosses to the locker and finds a jar of peanuts, which she opens, sniffs, and puts down. "What's a cave?"

"The Promised Land. At least, I think it is. That thing with Richard's knife—there's no way he could have known. No one knows. Just Patel. Now Suzy. But I think that's where they're headed. I figured you knew. I thought maybe you told Richard."

Miley stands perfectly still. He has the impression she's listening with every cell, every follicle. The painting his future wife sent came with a note that read, "In some cultures, if you build someone a house they own you." He'd never known whether she'd made that up.

"I want people to remember this show," he says, staring at Miley's back, one strap of her dress askew. He can't stop thinking of the lava lamp in Boby's office. "I want them to look back and talk about it, argue about what it meant. I want it to be worthy of everyone's sacrifice."

The sequence has begun to shape itself in his mind: One by one they would come into the cave, sit in its breathing darkness. A single camera. No cuts, no wipes, no music. Just the all-present darkness and the sense he'd felt of others having been there before— people he'd never meet, whose lives he couldn't imagine, who had brought to that cave the desperation and loneliness that still hung in the stale air. Even the Deserted would feel it—they had to feel it. Somehow that uncaring dark would bring them face to face with themselves, with whatever real selves they had left.

"Then what?" Miley asks.

"I haven't figured that out yet."

She opens the peanut jar again, fishes one out with a finger and rolls it around in her mouth. "Let me work on it. Boby will take some convincing—"

"No!" he says, his voice echoing on cold concrete. "No Boby."

"Look, you can't just go cowboy in Week Seven. Especially not if we're live—"

"This is where it's going. I don't give a flying fuck what Boby thinks about it."

Miley squints at him, then spits the tiny peanut at his feet. They both stare at it. Seven years, he thinks. He's always known that Miley would sit in his chair one day. But after all that time, he still can't say for sure if that's what she's after, or which master she really serves.

She checks her BlackBerry again, taps her nose absently with a finger. "You're the boss," she says. Then, brightly, "Looks like we're clear. Got your galoshes?"

When she opens the iron cover, a blast of sunshine needles into the backs of his eyes, a warm breeze swirling and kicking the wrappers and cigarette butts into a small cyclone on the concrete floor. After a series of explosive sneezes, he starts to climb, stopping on the second rung when he looks up inadvertently into the shadows under Miley's dress.

She looks down at him, her face lit once again with incandescent allure. "See something you like?"

Like another sneeze, grim misgiving shudders through him; rung by rung, they move back to the surface, his legs heavier with each step. By the time he's near the top, he's sure he's seen through it: there was no tsunami, the whole thing was an elaborate ploy to get him out of the action, sideline him, pump him for information.

They were whores. All of them.

The lava lamp glows in his imagination, red and viscous and bubbling in Boby's corner.

But when he tops the last rung, rests his arms atop the concrete silo, he's blinded by scimitars of light clanging off acres of standing water. Tangles of brush and driftwood, a tire from one of the golf carts, assorted articles of clothing, a dense school of red apples float past in wheeling, pointless currents. As Miley wades off, dress hiked to her hips, the producer shields his eyes against the glare and surveys this bright, incomprehensible landscape. He can't remember the way to his trailer. The jungle is silent—too silent, he thinks, easing one leg into the chill, his calf muscles cramping, chest tight, struck as if for the first time by the real meaning of "cancellation."

For three days he waits, all but incapacitated by anxiety, the sense of invisible gears turning everywhere. Boby's phone calls and emails have stopped. Paco and Patel are barely speaking to him. When the water level goes down, he tries to make the rounds of the Facility, reconnect with the crew, boost morale, but he's greeted with perfunctory cheer, a corporate briskness that barely masks their disgust. Walking past Engineering one afternoon, he sees Hector flip him off from the doorway; swelled with grief, he ducks into the fitness center, locks himself in a sauna, and cranks the steam until he's soaked through.

Only Miley keeps up a semblance of normalcy, the pretense of continuing respect. She goes about her job with a renewed breeziness, the same flawless competence he's prized for years. But her smiles no longer reassure him. Though he still sits in the chair, though the machinery of the show still responds to his commands, he's all too aware that he's on his own, as alone as any of the Deserted, struggling through the island's uncaring hellscape.

They've cleared the meteor crater, picked their way down to the salt flats, shuffled and stumbled their way to the very edge of the Mangrove Swamp. Richard lies in his litter, babbling paranoiacally, every so often growing lucid enough to draw another blood map before losing consciousness. The producer watches from his quarters and grinds his teeth. Each morning he lurches from the bed, gripped by the nauseating certainty that Gloria is gone—swept out to sea, struck down by plague, murdered in her sleep. He finds her on the monitors, retraces her movements, squeezes his stone until his palm throbs. Somehow their fates are connected—if they get rid of her it won't be long before he, too, is gone, evicted from his chair, stripped of his login codes, banished. Even the island seems to be slipping from his grasp, unexplained incidents coming one after another: fields of wildflowers blooming off-schedule; source-less plumes of smoke on the horizon; stars in the wrong place in the sky.

His rain-scented mist has run dry. Yoga is no longer an option. Only Armand could talk him off the ledge, but the old queen hasn't answered his phone for days. Finally, just before midnight, a connection—an old woman's voice gabbling in Spanish. He can only pick out a single word: *hospital*.

He tries to ask why—*¿Por que?*—but it comes out *Por favor*. "Por favor? Por favor . . ." he says, but doesn't know what comes next. After another burst the line goes dead.

If he were there, the producer would tell Armand he thinks his career is over. Not because of Boby, not because of his APs' treachery—but because he's lost his bearings, his vision. He can't keep it all straight: the changing alliances, the proliferating forks of possibility, nuances of angle and juxtaposition. Once upon a time he knew how to surf those tides of conflicting motives, fickle desires, how to organize, to find a story that was satisfying and plausible and absolutely organic. Reality was an empty canvas awaiting his brush. Now he stands before the show like a drooling child considering some unthinkably complex puzzle. His instrument is out of tune, dulled to the point of uselessness. He's become just another tool.

And he would tell Armand that he was right, that it is a comfort—but not in the way he'd thought. People didn't want to see themselves, they wanted to see someone else, someone bigger than them, someone in charge. That was the comfort: that in all the chaos someone was in control. And all the millions of people watching could sense it—even if they couldn't articulate their need, they felt it—and in that sensing they saw that the sudden misfortunes, the unpredictable calamities and minor inconveniences and galling reversals were not random. The squalor of their lives, the letdowns and uncontrolled furies, the frustrated dreams, the friends and lovers who betrayed them or who simply disappeared, the partners who stole from them, the smug and ungrateful sons who refused to understand them, the spouses who drifted away, the babies who died in the womb, the thousand daily ways in which life disappointed all efforts to make it worth living—they saw that all of it, however unbearable, happened according to someone's plan. Never mind if that someone was cruel, capricious, distant as computer-generated constellations. He was there. It was all that mattered.

On the wall of his quarters glow six gray faces, isolated from one another, all blinking up into starlight. No one is sleeping: not Hiroko, who drifts through the trees in an Ophelia-like daze; not Richard, who hours ago rose from his litter and led the others into the Mangrove Swamp. The producer logs into the system, enters commands to search the day's phone logs, scan the chats, boot the GPS, hoping to divine something from the vectors and hues of computerized symbols, catch some glimpse of a bigger picture.

But the system returns a strange message: ACCESS DENIED.

For an hour, he sits in full lotus, palms turned up, thumbs touching forefingers, until his legs are numb, his third eye bloodshot, until the futility of every other course becomes clear. Then he shuts down the monitors, turns on every light in the trailer. He makes the bed, washes a few glasses, polishes the teak showcase and every stone it contains. He opens all the windows, flooding his quarters with the jungle's night sounds; he dusts shelves, clears cobwebs, sweeps out the meditation space until the trailer shows no signs of having been lived in—only clean lines, shadowless corners, an emptiness that rattles behind him when he flings the flimsy door wide and walks out.

By moonrise, he's passed from jungle to broad, rolling prairie, traveling swiftly under a thin and shocking light. His breath comes out in steaming gusts, his leg muscles, so long deprived of yoga, quiver and cramp. The ground is dry and solid, the island's interior untouched by the tsunami. Keeping the dark mountains always ahead, he pushes on until the hills drop to a smooth swath of river—the mighty Canqaxim'po, miles downstream of the ruins. He can just make out the landing where, weeks or eons ago, they'd pulled Simon from the water and started him on the long journey home. He follows the near bank as the water ruffles and rushes, until land squeezes the river tight enough that he's able to ford, sputtering and slipping, dragging himself onto the far shore trailing river slime, his shoes filled with silt. Soon he's reached the western edge of the sand dunes, still radiating the day's heat; far to the east the night sky glows and shimmers above the Volcanic Labyrinth, where Candy met her end, and which Enviro estimates will take four to five months to cool completely. But this landscape, this ground across which he hurriedly travels, has no memory of Candy or Simon or any of the others; they came, they acted out their unthinkably small parts, they vanished, and the island never so much as blinked.

Avoiding the ice flats, he drops into a series of winding gulches, rough hillsides rising steadily until the night sky is a ribbon of algorithmic glitter, the producer a minute shadow far below. He emerges into a surreal and unfamiliar wood, thousands of blackened, leafless trees standing in regular rows, rank and file, stretching across his vision like so many burned toothpicks. He has no memory of this place, no clue how it got here. He slows to a walk as he crosses this blasted forest over which hangs a sense of tragedy, commanding deference. The air has grown colder; the ground rises steadily, all the northern sky bounded by the looming mountains, the moon over the highest peaks. There is no other way, he reminds himself constantly—the chain of command is compromised, the machine breaking down, storyboards in splinters. The show was his creation. It cannot live without him. He doesn't know whether what he's doing is genius or foolhardiness, only that unless he does something the show will crumple into itself and vanish from memory, just one more thing that should have lasted, should have meant something, but didn't. And all that will remain then is the Show, a perversion of everything they'd set out to do, a series of interchangeable puppet dances obscuring and obliterating the real—until, inevitably, it had taken the place of the real and in so doing, become real.

By the time the setting moon gives way to pale pink, he's shin-deep in the Mangrove Swamp's southern edge. The air reeks of methane and rich animal odors that gather in the back of his throat. Fatigue crawls on his face like a cowl. His movements are slowed by floating vines like the thick tresses of some woodland witch, by submerged roots that trap his ankles; the squelching sound his legs make is gruesome, bodily. Something slithers past his knee and he stumbles, plunges an arm into the muck; when he stands it whips past him along the surface of the water and he forces a fist into his mouth to keep from crying out, tasting the swamp's brackish, ancient filth.

Carefully, he plods through the steamy archipelago of ridges and banks, now stopping to listen for voices, now sniffing at the pungent air. He is a pair of eyeballs that float haltingly atop the sluggish water. Unseen birds cackle at each other in the weakening dark; owls hoot; monkeys screech. At last, through the tangle of shadows, he sees a spark, a human form crossing in and out of fire-light. He approaches with a cautious, sculling motion, drapes an arm over the blade of a banyan root, breathes into the crook of his elbow while his legs float dead and distorted below.

On a hillock of humus and tangled roots, Richard lies semiconscious in his litter, babbling at the trees. His wounded leg is enormous, encrusted with soaked bandages. Bloody drool trails from his chin. A green sheet hangs on a branch over his head; when it flutters in the wind the hairdresser cries out, flings an arm as if to ward off a threat. In a moment Bernatelli emerges from the brush carrying a ski pole on which is speared a chunk of pale, oozing meat. His jeans are spattered with blood, his forearms black with it. He squats by the fire, extends the pole into the flame, prompting a long, pitiful wail from the litter. Though the producer has studied their files, watched hundreds of hours of tape, in the flesh the two men look strange to him, small and awkward; the shadows thrown by their movements confuse his eye. Bernatelli's biceps seem, suddenly, human; when he coughs, the ex-Marine almost seems fragile.

The producer holds still as a wave of greasy, bitter smoke drifts across the water. He has to submerge himself in the swamp to keep from choking on it. Richard rails unintelligibly, kicking his good leg against the edge of the litter. "Try to get some shut-eye," says Bernatelli—his voice, too, reduced, just one among the swamp's myriad sounds, nearly lost in the mix. He rips a bite of meat from the ski pole, bares his teeth in the hairdresser's direction, juice shining a slick down his chin. Richard bawls again, and all at once the producer recognizes the jade kimono billowing on the branch, understands the strangled name the hairdresser keeps repeating: *Hiroko!*

It takes every ounce of yogic control to move off from the banyan and float back into the swamp—his heart banging painfully, his throat seizing as if he were being force-fed from Bernatelli's spear. When he can no longer see the campfire, he lowers his face to the water, opens his mouth and tries to scream, comes up choking, shivering, the terrible gamey smell lodged in his sinuses, sinking into the tissue of his soft palate.

"What the fuck was that?" someone says, too close. He drops into a crouch, ducks back into a tangle of vegetation. Peering through the vines he sees Alejandra, standing at the water's edge, hands on hips, naked except for fishnet stockings and a leather collar. "Walter?" she calls, scanning the gray. "You come and bother me, you know what you get, Walt. ¿Me entiendes?" Floating on his stomach, the producer creeps closer, lifts his eyes above a mossy log to find Shaneequio, spread-eagled and tied to stakes by rawhide straps. The math teacher returns to stand over him, flicking Shaneequio's switchblade and snapping it closed, flicking it and closing it while the gang counselor moans, his cock rising like some rare, poisonous swamp creature. Again the producer has trouble recognizing them, can't quite match them to the lookalikes on his monitors. Their skin seems swollen, mottled; the sounds they make are uncomfortably close.

"Puta," Alejandra spits. "You little puta," squatting over Shaneequio and holding the knife to his throat. "I hate you, puta, I never love you," she says, panting in clouds while she urinates on Shaneequio's chest. She brings her face close to his, snarling in ecstasy, drooling into his eyes. "You ruin my life. I hate you, puta, you ruin my life!"

The producer pulls himself hand over hand along the mossy log, barely able to keep from sinking into the murk. He can see himself, lying below the scum, below tangled roots and the floating carcasses of centuries of blind creatures, stretched out in a final, incomparable shavasana.

He squeezes past toppled trees moist with fungus, through a shallow pond covered with lily pads, through a long arbor of thorns that tear at face and scalp. It was his absence, of course. Peering into dark passages, he thinks no hardship or humiliation could matter to them as much as his absence. That he would bring them to such a place and then leave them to determine their own purpose, meet their own fate. What kind of vision was that? To let them think they were alone, that he no longer cared what happened to them—it wasn't vision; it was cruelty. Of course they hated him. They were the Deserted.

On the other side of a massive anthill, Gloria Hamm kneels on a moss bank, hunched over a bucket, her back to the producer. She's shirtless, whistling to herself, a plaintive melody that blends with the swamp's sickly light. He listens for a time, stares at her slumped shoulders, studies every vertebra along the unlovely, mole-dappled ridge of her back. Without fill lights, her figure is complicated by shadows; without backlights, the swamp seems poised to swallow her whole. Inch by sodden inch he pulls himself onto land. An owl hoots and Gloria tilts her head as though thinking of something sweetly sad. Her meandering tune starts and stops, exquisitely out of place. The producer stands dripping only yards away and waits for her to notice.

Who is this woman? Why can't he get her out of his thoughts? He knows her every blemish, her every peculiarity of hygiene. The sight of her bare, wiggling foot entrances him; the sound of her spitting toothpaste brings on a fit of restlessness no sun salutation can assuage. His nights are filled with images of her—and yet all that has passed between them are flickers of glass and electrode, tingles of current, invisible signals. Though he has traveled across hostile terrain to find her, he understands, staring at her back, that he doesn't know her at all—this dour woman who puts her fingers into strangers' mouths, picks beneath their gums with pointed tools. He feels a sharp envy for those patients who have tasted her skin, for the intimacy of that toothy communion.

For five weeks she's refused to play, but even Gloria can't help being swept into the narrative, can't hide from its weather. She's in danger now, he can feel it—whether from Paco's machinations or the abuse of the other players or the island's inexplicable vagaries, its looming malice. And from the hard logic of the show itself: If she can't be useful, she'll end up on the skiff. But she doesn't know how to be useful. She only knows how to be herself.

But who is she?

When the owl hoots again, he steps behind her, pulse racing. His fingertips hover above her bare shoulders. Gloria stiffens but doesn't turn. Over her shoulder he can see what she sees: the bucket nearly full, her watery reflection marked with darkness.

He wants to say her name—*Gloria!*—but finds his jaw unwilling. His tongue has trouble moving over his teeth; his lips press too tightly to form the word.

Gloria! he tries again. His fingertips ache to touch her. Her dark hair tangled at the nape of her neck, her shoulder blades mannish, slightly lopsided. The smell of her body drifts up to him, faintly sour. He breathes from the bottom of his diaphragm, forces air past his larynx but can't make a sound. Overhead, too close, the owl hoots again—in the back of his mind he wonders about spycams and boundary mics, but he doesn't care about that, or anything but the woman before him, her face doubled in the bucket. He leans forward, tries to put his own face into the frame, but there's only a black, floating shape troubling the image, the stunned blinking of her eyes.

Gloria, he wills himself to say, pressure cinching his stomach, his testicles—*Gloria!* He drops to his knees; his mouth is filled with her name but sound won't come, only the eerie cry of the owl, the murmurs of the Mangrove Swamp. He snakes his arms around her middle, presses his face to her back—but Gloria doesn't move, even when he starts to squeeze. He closes his eyes, feels the clammy chill of her skin against his cheek, the rough scabs across her midriff, her quickening breath, listens to the distant, alien thumping of her heart.

It's a priceless tableau, full of pathos and peril. Just look at that contrast, the shadows shifting just so. Gloria Hamm, dental hygienist, one of five remaining players, stares entranced at her own reflection while the producer, soaked and begrimed, trailing all manner of sodden plant life, clutches her body, mouth opening and closing in mute frustration. It's like nothing you've ever seen—or ever wanted to see. You can't pretend to know what it means, only watch in queasy distaste as the swamp sky lightens and, too fast to make them out, the credits start to roll.

WEEK SIX

∎

. . . previously

The doctors taught him the term "cervical incompetence," to explain why her body would not hold a baby for more than three months. As the embryo grew, the pressure mounted, until one day, without warning—while she was painting, or getting a manicure, or browsing for nursing bras—the tiny donut of muscle gave way and flushed fluid and blood and an invisible child to whom they'd learned not to give a name. The first time it happened he was in the Maghreb and could not get back for almost three weeks. When he came home he found every room in the house repainted, punk rock blaring from a tune box on the back patio. His wife had set her easel up by the pool and was painting canvasses of the smog—tight, magnified images of grainy darkness hovering over the unsuspecting homes below. After that they timed it carefully, planning around the show's inexorable cycle. But the off-season was no luckier; a little over a year later he found himself sitting next to her hospital bed, hunched on a wobbly, four-wheeled stool, holding her hand while she bawled inconsolably. He said what he could to comfort her, but he knew they were just words, and worse—they were words with a purpose, meant to bring a smile to her face, to give her hope, to relieve from his shoulders the burden of her misery. After Patagonia they tried cerclage, but she started spotting within days, and then it was over, and he was next to her again in an identical hospital room on what he could have sworn was the same broken stool. This time she was dry-eyed; he pressed his forehead to the back of her hand and murmured many of the same things he'd said the last time, hoping to make one of them believe it would be alright. He could hear the repetition—the forced optimism, the platitudes—as though he were recycling the lines, as though—and this thought hit him like a fist, dried his tears instantly—he were reading from a script. He saw himself then, as though he were looking through the door of the hospital room: playing the role of the good husband, being there for his wife, mourning the child they'd lost, the child it was increasingly seeming they would never have. Through the door of the hospital room he watched these two people behave exactly as two people in that situation would behave. It was, he knew, a good scene. From there it was a short jump to think of other parts of their lives—whisking through the lobby of the Four Seasons Milan, tossing the keys to a valet at Chateau Marmont, inspecting fruit at the farmers market, even sitting by the pool with the Sunday *Times*, all these little performances, virtuoso imitations of things he'd observed, things he'd read about, or some bodiless ideal of how such things should be done. He'd stood with her on a bluff on the Pacific Palisades, Armand at his side, and repeated words that came not from his heart but from a minister's laminated card—never mind that the words corresponded accurately enough to his feelings, to the commitment he wanted to make: they were just words, symbolic and insufficient, an affront to true emotion. And wasn't it all like that? The way he treated his crew—learned from the producers he himself had worked for, or seen working, or characters in movies about movies. His drink—single malt in a brandy snifter—where had he picked it up? Even driving his Corvette, the way he imagined himself winding into the canyon, the way he cranked the volume and leaned into the curves, seeing himself in the most generic of music videos. The cut of his suit, the way he nodded his approval to a sommelier, his florid signature, how he snapped the pages of the newspaper before folding it—where, he thought now, was his true self, that unique and authentic part of him that was born the instant he was born, that was not merely a copy? Was there any part of his life that was not an act? He thought then of his father, driving those hot and empty highways for weeks at a time, beaming with pride as he demonstrated the beauty and effectiveness of his hammers. He thought of those years after his father's death when he could not go outside without risking the asphyxiating panic, and how he'd pushed back that panic with a word—unintelligible, without meaning, spoken over and over, volubly, in public. Had even the word been an act? For sure, it had started as a spontaneous outpouring, a pressure valve. But the looks on people's faces—kindness, pity, disgust—became a strange enticement, and he couldn't be sure anymore he hadn't done it on purpose, just to get that reaction, to get any reaction at all from the strangers around him, the multitudes who would not otherwise notice his existence, or notice if that existence suddenly ended. For weeks, months, these thoughts consumed him. He second-guessed his every action, his simplest daily habits. In every word he spoke he heard the deafening echoes of its unoriginality, the repetition that drained it of value. The house was silent as he and his wife each nursed their private terror. They tried once more after that, a year or two later, while he was recovering from Benin—but in his mind that was the last time, the end of some innocent era in which they lived life as a kind of joint project, something they were building, together, from scratch, and not merely the pointless and predetermined scrabbling of ants, two of a trillion identical organisms flashing into the gene pool for long enough to reproduce—or not—and then die. There comes a time in every man's life when he takes stock of himself, where he's been and where he's going, a time when he sets a path and lets nothing and nobody thwart him from his cherished goals. And so, after six long weeks, they find themselves in the darkest heart of the island's treacherous swamp, just days from Paradise Beach and the spectacular finale where one will earn the title, Lord of the Island. Five weary travelers, haunted by what they've been through, unsure who to trust. They don't know what last ordeals stand between them and victory. Or that somewhere on the island, someone still watches, waiting to wreak an age-old revenge. Which one of the Deserted has got what it takes? Don't go away.

Every leaf, every root, every perfect grain of dirt. Every termite mound, every cacao pod, every giant hissing beetle. Every snake and chameleon, every shrieking parrot, chirring locust, growling sloth, every flopping bullfrog, praying mantis, every creeping, glistening slug. Every stinging, flying, humming thing. Every scent of eucalyptus, every weeping banyan, every flash of a toucan's tail. Every rustle and every moan, every crack of thunder, every desolate howl in the dead of night. Every strange creaking exhalation of this stinking swamp lost to the maps. Everything has been noted, logged, tested, run through models, plugged into spreadsheets. That which fell short of standards has been enhanced. What could not be enhanced has been eliminated. Nothing on the island is unknown, nothing outside the producer's ken. He is to the swamp as he would be to his own pool shed. As he *has been* to his own pool shed: kneeling in darkness, surrounded by wet, muffled noises, unsure of his next move.

What does he want to tell her? In all the weeks he's thought of Gloria Hamm, the hours spent staring at her image, he's never thought what he would do if he met her, never imagined the dampness of her skin against his face, the soft flab encircled by his arms, the irresistible push of her breath. Only the imperative: to stand in the same space, breathe the same air. To be sure they both existed, that they could exist simultaneously, to cross the threshold of camera and monitor and bring those existences, those realities, together—and let no man or woman then cut them asunder.

And to protect her from whatever is coming—to be, at last, what she would want him to be: sword and shield against this world and its dangers. To fulfill the promise he made, or should have made. To make himself useful.

Gloria stares at her reflection in the bucket. The swamp holds still. Even the owl has stopped its mad hooting. Silence squeezes his very bones, rattles in the hollows of his cold, yoga-deprived joints.

"Life out here is hard," she finally says. "You have to be ready for anything." Her voice is tired but uneasy, stilted and overeager. The producer holds still as her belly pushes against his arms.

"There are bugs. And wild animals! And it's so hot . . ." She sighs, looks up into the canopy, clears her throat. "Everything's stacked up against you. You can't eat, or sleep," she says, warming to the speech, "you have to watch your back. Someone's always got it in for you. You have to be smarter, faster, stronger . . ." She stops to think. "And the food's disgusting. I would kill someone for a Starbucks. And I mean *kill* . . ."

As quickly as it began, the burst of energy peters out and she goes slack in his arms again. The producer turns his face until the tip of his nose touches the warm spot his cheek made on her back. Her name swells at the root of his tongue. "You can't trust anyone!" she says without conviction. She shakes her head, mutters to herself, tries again: "They're out to get you. I know, the way they look at me. Even Richard. Even Alejandra"—she hesitates—"that bitch!"

The swamp crowds in on them, as if every tree and vine hung on her words. "This is ridiculous," she mumbles. He wants to tell her to stop, that this isn't what he needs, but his throat is too hot.

"Don't get to know anyone," she says, louder. "Other people are the enemy. Don't make friends, don't trust anyone or look out for them. That's how you lose. Those people all made one mistake: They got involved with each other. That's how you get fucked. Look at Stan," she says. "Nobody stood up for him, did they? Clarice? Hiroko, with her little schemes. Where is she now? She's dinner.

"Not me. You gotta play it safe. Don't talk. Don't listen. No alliances, no rivalries. Those stars up there," she says, looking up into the canopy, "they're billions of miles apart. And they live forever."

A frog croaks in the silent swamp. Gloria slumps forward. "That's the best I can do," she says. "I don't know what else you want me to say."

The producer holds her body tightly. It's somehow miraculous, this body; he is amazed by its solidity, its warmth, by the undeniable fact of it.

"Just get rid of me already," she says. "Get it over with. I don't know why you've kept me here. Must be some kind of joke." She laughs a quiet, bitter laugh. "Watch the heavy girl try to climb a tree. Look at the fat girl hanging out with the beauty queens. Is she stupid enough to think she can win?"

Gloria shrugs out of his embrace and climbs to her feet. "You think I don't know? I come all the way out here and put up with these people—you think I don't get it? One morning you'll come and get me, and then everyone gets to laugh when the fat girl realizes she never stood a chance. How funny! Look how crushed she is. What else does she have to live for?"

From somewhere in the swamp comes a man's cry of pain. Somewhere in the canopy, a red light blinks and bobs like a strange, iridescent firefly. A rumble rises in the producer's throat. Daylight is coming to the Mangrove Swamp, seeping between branches, troubling the murky water.

"And you people get off on it." Gloria stands over him, arms crossed over her chest. "What kind of people are you? You make us look like idiots. You make us act crazy, do these terrible things. And why? Just to see that little camera light turn on. Just to get your attention. We do all of it for your attention. And you totally get off on it. You're disgusting," she says. "Even Bernatelli has more integrity than you do."

On his knees in the wet moss, the producer reaches for Gloria but she backs away. "What do you want?" she says. "You win, okay? I came this far. Just tell me what you want and let's get it over with."

Exhaustion pulls at his every muscle. Cold hunger has taken root in his belly; a hot grip squeezes his throat. Squinting, Gloria takes a step forward and drops her arms, bares her body. "Is this what you want?"

A dull grunt slips from his lips. Gloria's breasts are large and heavy, one badly damaged, dimpled and irregular, carved along its outer curve as though something had taken a bite out of it. His teeth start to chatter; his eyes sting in the swamp's noxious air.

"Do I have your attention now?" She leans toward him, until he can see her mocking smile. "If this is what it takes, fine. You know why? Because I'm a winner."

The producer's tongue prickles; his ribs ache with the effort of speech. Gloria stands inches away, so close it's overwhelming, vaguely sickening: her flesh, veined and marked, stippled with chill; the rough sound of her breath; her heavy smell. Her thighs are broad; her belly sags over the cinched rope she wears as a belt. Three or four long, dark hairs wind below her navel. It's worse than high definition: every blemish and mole visible, every stretch mark and wrinkle, every knob of bone, every keloid, every rough and scaly patch of skin insists on his attention. Her ruined breast looms like a long-rotted fruit, hollowed out and collapsed.

"Tell me what to do," she says. "I'm a winner. Give me another week." Still he doesn't move. "Come on, big guy. Show me how to win." She touches the back of her hand to his cheek. Her voice is honey and acid, her eyes metal. "I'm right here," she says, pressing her palm to his face. "I'm the real thing. You want to touch me? Do it. I'm a winner."

The producer shakes his head until his ears ring, but she doesn't back away. "What's the matter, big guy? You afraid? Come on, show me how to be a winner." Shivering, the producer reaches into his pocket, squeezes the small stone in his fist.

"Let's go, big guy, give me some attention," she says. "Show me how—"

"*Na*—" he belches, every muscle clenched around the stabbing heat in his throat.

"What's that?" she says. "You want to fuck me? Go for it, big guy. Fuck me."

"*Guh*—" he retches, the pain lurching him forward onto hands and knees, his nose close to her unshaved shins, the stone hard and cold in his fist. "*Guh*—"

"Go ahead, fuck me, big guy," she says. Behind her, two bright red lights weave lower between the trees. "You want me to lie down? You want me to lean against that tree? Just tell me. I'm a winner."

One by one, the sounds rise into his throat—razor-edged consonants, vowels packed in phlegm, diphthongs lewd and nauseous—scraping against his tonsils, slicking sour across the back of his tongue. A buzzing has arisen in his ears.

"Just tell me what you want," Gloria says, baring her teeth. "Want me to jack you off? Want to come on my face? I'm a winner. Whatever it takes, right?"

His noise gains volume and force, surging out of some dark vault in his chest, its cover weakened with time and finally blown off. Barks and babbles, pitiful whimpers, sick choking sounds tear at his trachea—he can't breathe, his nose stuffed; panic traces a cold line from the back of his neck down to his anus. With his last ounce of control, he holds the small stone out to Gloria, as if this could make the burning noise stop. She peers at the stone, wary at first, then starts to laugh.

"What's that? You want to put that inside me? You want to fuck me with that?" She has to shout over the garbled sounds he's making. "Whatever, big guy! Let's go already. I'll bend over, that what you want?" He shakes his head like an imbecile, spits more meaningless jabber. Her mouth comes close to his face, her breath gamey and sweet. "You want me on all fours? Want to work your fist in there? Fine. Do it! I am a winner."

Another volley of gibberish sears his throat with bile. The owl has started hooting again; harried birds scream in alarm. The swamp swarms with red lights. The producer thrusts the stone at Gloria, but she closes her fist over his. "There's no time, big guy," she says through gritted teeth. "Shut up and tell me what you want."

Tears leak from the corners of his eyes. Still babbling, he tries to pull his hand away. "My ass?" she says. "Is that it? You want to fuck my ass?" She yanks at her rope belt. "Whatever, okay? I'm a winner. Shut up and fuck my ass. Do what you gotta do. You want to smack me? You want to choke me?" she says. "Just get it over with! You want to cut me? Burn me? How do I know what kind of weird shit you want? But you know what? I don't care. Because I'm a winner," she says. "It's all the same to me."

The awful sounds won't stop, the pain in his chest forcing them out. In desperation he pulls her wrist toward his face, opens his mouth, and forces both of their hands between his teeth. Startled, she tries to pull away, but he tightens his grip and opens wider. He feels her bones against the hard roof of his mouth, her fingernails on the meat of his tongue.

"Stop," she whispers, wide-eyed. But he can't stop. He's gagging on Gloria's hand, his vision starting to shimmer and darken, the senseless, primitive sounds stopped up at last. When her hand can't go any farther, knuckles resting against the soft tissue of his throat, he closes his eyes and tries mightily to swallow.

But then: sudden noises behind him, a swishing of swamp grass, a snapping of twigs. Voices. Panicked, choking, he searches Gloria's face. He knows from her expression what he'll find when he turns around: the end of his career—a thought that brings a gust of relief as he tries, too late, to climb to his feet. He has barely an instant to register Bernatelli's face looming huge from the mist, behind him a battery of floodlights, boom mics, one Fresnel spot glaring from atop a crane, before the ex-Marine's fist smashes into the producer's face, knocking him ass-backward, mercifully mute, into the island's welcoming muck.

Cue the coyote: baying in triumph as the screen goes to black.

"What is love?"

It's simple. So simple that the discovery is accompanied by embarrassment—how could he not have understood until now?

"What is love?" Of course! It was the obvious choice, clear and provocative as a Zen koan but better: something everyone was sure they knew the answer to, until they were actually asked the question, until they actually had to speak it aloud.

They would enter the cave, one at a time—no tiki torches, no pipe organ or voice-over, just their own fear and disorientation, and a dark space full of guano and the presence of generations of vanished inhabitants who'd huddled there for safety and warmth.

They'd go in without expectations, without promise of reward, and once they'd passed beyond the entrance's lingering light a voice would ask, "What is love?" and until they answered honestly, until they said something unpracticed, unironic, without bravado or hidden agenda, something that exposed them as the lonely, confused, terrified people that deep down they had to be, they would not be allowed to leave.

"What is love?" A question that should prompt outpourings, inspire poetry, odes to the power of the ineffable, that should bring out the truest face of our uncorrupted nature—but which in reality is considered impolite, vaguely shameful, like farting in the opera: a disruption of all the encrusted conventions that permit the world to function, that keep us from collapsing into wails of grief or hacking one another to bits at the slightest provocation. There would be embarrassment, bewilderment, revulsion. When they heard the question, when they understood they had no choice but to answer honestly, there would be anger—yes, they would be angry at being confronted this way, at having their painstakingly constructed personas stripped from them. But they would answer.

Oh, yes, they would answer.

Not walks on the beach. Not a many-splendored thing. Not a rose in spring or the laughter of a child or a candlelight dinner or Angelina Fucking Jolie. Not helping an old woman cross the street. Not the ties that bind, whatever that means. Not a box of chocolates or a diamond necklace or multiple orgasms or a surprise weekend getaway to Canyon Ranch. Not a sunset. Not a Robert Doisneau photograph (though he, too, had hung that print in his bedroom in Venice, a lifetime ago). Not quiet mornings or nights of unbridled passion or a nose wrinkled in adorable laughter or a set of powerful shoulders or a fuel-injected V-8. Not a Carnival cruise. Not a Cape Cod sunrise. Not what we'll remember. Not blindness. Not *la petite mort*. Not the pitter-patter of little feet or the burst of fireworks in a summer sky. Not a Michelin star or a stroll along the Seine, not a sweaty palm or a sidelong glance or a come-hither look or a pat on the back. Not cleavage. Not muscle. Not real estate. Not sunshine or sea spray, not massage oil, not Viagra, not a head on the shoulder or a hand on the knee, not a peck on the cheek, a tuxedo, a veil, not mussed hair, not spandex, not Lexus or Maybelline. Not the Virgin Islands. Not the Four Seasons. Not Punta del Este or winters in Chamonix. Not Taos. Not mariachi. Not Sinatra, not Kennedy, not King. Not the billowing stars and stripes and not apple pie. Not Grandma. Not Gatorade. Not a warm fire on Christmas, a snowstorm, a cloudburst, not the perfect wave, not fresh-squeezed OJ. Not life insurance. Not homeowner's insurance. Not Toys 'R Us or Budweiser beer. Not email. Not voicemail. Not talking birthday cards or a new washer-dryer. Not Rohl faucets or a Viking range, not Klipsch speakers, not an Aeron chair, not water jets or surround sound, not feather down, not central air. Not blue sky. Not gray sky. Not weather. Not God.

He would not accept cant or cliché, would not settle for advertising slogans. No, they would stay in that cave—alone, unaided, with no time limit on this last, crucial ordeal—until they said something original, something that came from whatever was left of their authentic selves. Until they said one goddamned thing that was true.

After that, for all he cares, they could waterski off the back of a submarine or wrestle with jaguars or slice each other to ribbons with razor blades—whatever Boby wants, whatever Paco and Miley decide between them, he won't stand in their way. They could finish out the season, cancel the series, go on to their next projects, however childish and demeaning of human existence they might be. He's done. He would watch the finale and then pack up his remaining rocks and take the next network plane back to Jakarta. He would skip the reunion. He would forgo the celebration at the Dubai Tower—no absinthe, no strippers, no blow—fly commercial back to L.A. and retire. He would sell the condo in Mumbai, put the key near St. Barts in trust. He would drain the swimming pool, rip out the bougainvillea, take his suits to Goodwill, close up all but a few rooms in the house in Laurel Canyon, start cooking for himself again. He would wait for the show, all thirteen years of it, to fade from his memory and his every unconscious reflex, and then he would stand by the empty pool and stare over the wall at the vast, smoggy city, the endless plains of apartments and bungalows with all their beetling, teeming life, the crazed arterial freeways and the airplanes queued up silently in the sky and beyond it all the gleaming, infinite ocean, and figure out what to do next.

Until then, he'll do yoga.

He has little choice in the matter. Punishment has been swift and precise: his keys taken from him, his entry codes cancelled. Since they dragged him back from the swamp, woozy and weak-legged, his clothes ruined, his nose broken, two guards have been stationed outside the trailer—large, bald men he'd never seen before. The command center is a forbidden country. His meals are delivered by one of the kitchen girls who blinks dark eyes at him and struggles to hold in a giggle; his emails, texts, IMs, and tweets disappear into a digital void. And yet the show goes forward. Week Seven looms. Intervention is no longer possible. He's finally lost control.

"Do you know who I am?" he'd blubbered, scrounging blindly in the swamp's mud and moss, desperately searching for the stone he'd lost. "Do you know who I am? Do you know who I am?" His eyes swam with blood and snot; his ears rang; all around him bodies jostled to get close, cameras in his face, Bernatelli kicking him in the ribs while he plunged his arms over and over into the dark weedy water. He'd felt Gloria there, watching him without pity as they hauled him to his feet. He could not look her in the eye. The footage has run every night on *Inside Edition* and *Entertainment Tonight*. It's been viewed millions of times on YouTube, an instant classic.

Day and night, his trailer is filled with muffled voices, the groans of machinery, unidentifiable crashes, rumbles, slams from outside. He sits in full lotus and tries to slow his pulse. He listens to Tibetan chants and drinks green tea. He reorganizes his rocks, arranges them by size, by color, by geologic period, by geographic origin. He takes them from the showcase and distributes them throughout the trailer: shiny chips of mica snaking across the meditation space; gray turtle-like loaves in the shower; a dazzling geode where his pillow used to be. Each morning he checks the shelves, as though his favorite stone might somehow turn up—but where it once sat there's only a faint outline, a fast-fading halo of dust.

He logs into the system using his new, severely restricted account, searches the database for *extraction, rejection, elimination, loss*. Scans through old sequences, splices together footage of players leaving the show—dozens of them, lost to avalanches or sunstroke or the predation of bears, to holes in the earth that opened without warning, debris that fell from the sky. How many ways had they devised to banish people, to show how heartlessly they could send one another away? But in thirteen years they've never even tried to show love. What kind of reality has he built?

"You could have at least fucked her," Miley says when she comes to see him, three days after his last urgent page. "You could have nailed her right there and then, instead of . . . what *were* you doing, getting a tonsillectomy? Or wait, let me guess: You had a really bad toothache."

The junior AP stands just inside the trailer's open door, as though wary of venturing too far inside. She leans, too casually, against the wall, hands deep in her pockets. The producer is inverted into a shoulder-stand, lumps of quartz arranged in a circle around him. He's never seen Miley look so uncomfortable—but this, too, is an act. He's almost sure of it.

"Like you couldn't get laid in the Facility? Half of HR has it in for you. Or the kitchen girls? Five minutes, you're pounding one of them in the deep freeze, hairnet and all."

Seen upside-down, Miley is oddly disproportional—top-heavy and pointy-chinned, the ghost of an overweight future almost visible in her hips. The scar at her jaw looks like a seam that holds her face together.

She nods to the guards outside and pulls the door shut with a click. "If I'd known you were that desperate, I guess I could have given you a handjob or something."

He crosses his legs in the air. "Not sure I could afford you," he says.

Her mouth opens in disbelief, closes in grim forbearance. "Do I deserve that?"

"Probably not."

The day after the mess in Benin, she'd arrived at the Facility, seeming to walk out of the dust cloud raised by a convoy of jeeps. "You don't have to think," she told him, when she found him locked inside an editing studio. She held him and spoke quietly. "You don't have to make any decisions until you're ready. Just stand next to me so they know you're still in charge, and I'll keep the show going. I'll make sure everyone knows what to do." He allowed her to lead him out of the studio and through the dining hut, where the silent crew huddled over bowls of relief rice and didn't look at one another. They lifted their heads when they saw him; they nudged one another and muttered. As he neared the exit, a PA started to clap; soon there was a standing ovation, ragged cheers and whistles, pounding on tables, and he knew everything would be alright.

But he should have seen it then: That was the day the show ceased to be his. What happened in Benin was a warning, a message about reality and whose prerogative it is to make reality. The network heard the message and responded accordingly.

"You don't have to worry," he tells her, letting his knees cramp down next to his ears, folding himself fetally until he can't see her anymore. "I'm not trying to escape. Tell your friends in Burbank, I just want to see it through. Then I'm done. Tell Paco. It'll be his show. He can do whatever he wants. I'm not interested—"

"Candy's dead," she says.

Slowly, he lets himself roll forward, flattening along the length of his back, flexing into fish pose. "Who?"

"Corporate lawyer? Blonde? Nasty as a pit bull?"

"Right. Of course she is. That was two weeks ago."

"No," Miley says, crossing the room to stand by his head. "I mean really dead. Deceased. When she fell in the labyrinth, she fractured her skull. The docs in Bangkok missed it. She had a brain bleed on the flight to Denver. The underwriters are going crazy. Network's trying to put it on the airline." The producer blinks up at her; somehow he can't make this information compute. "I thought you'd want to know," she says.

He struggles to his feet, legs wobbly. On the monitors, the montage keeps looping through: a woman leaving Greenland on a snowmobile; a man surrounded by wolves in Grand Teton; Clarice, sobbing on her pallet in the priestess's hut. In his mind he adds to it: Candy on a plane, flipping through a magazine, startled by a sudden pain.

And Hiroko. He doesn't even want to think about Hiroko.

"What now?" he says.

She shrugs extravagantly. "Who knows? They'll try to keep it quiet until after the finale." She stoops to examine a fist-sized chunk of obsidian he'd found in the bowl of an extinct volcano. "I'm just worried about the other players."

"Let's keep them off the airlines," he says.

"I meant what if they find out."

"I know what you meant."

Shadows clash outside the trailer's windows, disconnected from the rush of voices passing by. Coldplay's roadies arrived earlier by helicopter; since noon the sound checks have resounded through the Facility: the ethereal chime of guitars, monotonous snare beats pounding and echoing through the trees like drums of war. Not for the first time, he has the unsettling sense that if he left the trailer he wouldn't recognize what's out there, that this small, confined space—hardwood, spartan bed, wall dancing with bright images— is all he can really know, everything else ephemeral, illusory.

"Was it Patel?" he says.

"Was what Patel?"

"He was the only one who knew about the Promised Land. At least before I sent Suzy up there. How else would Richard have found out? I figure, I don't know, he sees the writing on the wall, sees you and Paco in line to take over—"

Miley laughs a bewildered, mirthless laugh. "I think you've done too many headstands. You think Patel would sell you out? Jesus," she says, wandering past the monitors, "like he doesn't have enough to deal with, with a sick baby and a depressed wife! Like he's looking for ways to stab you in the back."

"Right," he says, suddenly lightheaded, remembering the strange face on the test monitor, the empty gaze. How could he have forgotten about the baby? "Is it OK?"

"He thinks you're some kind of genius, don't you know that? He idolizes you." She brandishes the black rock at him. "Everyone around here idolizes you. Why do you think they fly around the world for you, devote their careers to you?"

He shrugs. "For the lasagna?"

"Fuck off," Miley says. "Have you thought for even one second about how disappointed people are in you?"

"People?"

"Fine: me."

He stands by the empty showcase, runs a finger along the edge of a shelf. "Yeah, I've thought of that."

He had not been able to cry in Nicaragua, had not allowed himself to break down in front of his crew. Then, back in L.A., there was post-production to supervise, a memorial service to endure. He'd gone to Puget Sound for solitude, but after the morning on the beach he'd hiked back to his tent with the smooth red stone in his pocket and waited for grief to blow him apart. He'd sat in the milky light of the old forest, and when he closed his eyes he saw himself: in close-up, in black-and-white, in an overhead dolly shot, in a majestic pan that conveyed his true insignificance. He'd waited for the tears to come, but in his mind he never could settle on the right angle.

"It's gotten away from us," he says. "Everything's so different from what it was supposed to be."

Miley tosses and catches the chunk of obsidian. "That's the thing," she says. "I don't really know what it was supposed to be. This idea of yours, this 'artistic vision'? Frankly, it never made much sense."

He considers this. "So much for believing in me."

She tosses the black rock, lets it fall and clatter against the hardwood, leaving a large, splintered divot by her foot. "That's something else I did for you: I pretended to believe in you." She picks up the obsidian and hands it to him. "I pretended to believe in you because I believed in you. I wonder if you can understand that."

"I think I can."

A knock comes at the trailer door and Miley opens it; one of the guards hands her a small parcel, which she inspects and tosses to the producer—his rain-scented mist refill, at long last sent by his yoga teacher.

With a last sigh, she starts out the door. "Well, good. Glad we got that settled. Have a nice life. I'll make sure you get this week's rushes, for old time's sake. The finale's going live, in case you missed that memo—"

"Do you still believe in me?" he says.

She stops in the doorway but doesn't look at him, smacks the aluminum siding with the flat of her hand. "What?"

"Do you?" He waits for her answer, looks down to where the chunk of rock hit the floor. Somehow it comes as a surprise that the hardwood overlay is only a quarter-inch thick; beneath it is ordinary plywood, sturdy as a house of cards. "Because I need your help."

On the island, the terrain has never been more hostile. The wind whips, the dust swirls. The tropical sun beats like a hammer on five figures making their way through the badlands—sandstone buttes like anvils, tormented columns of rock towering over them like gallows. The ground scattered with the skulls of dead scavengers. At the front of this grim procession, Bernatelli and Alejandra jostle for the lead, throwing elbows, scattering grit and scree underfoot. Every so often, the math teacher tugs on a leather cord tied to Shaneequio's ankle. Shaneequio and Gloria groan under the weight of Richard's litter, while the hairdresser lies paralyzed, staring into the merciless sun. The mountains rise before them. What awful secrets, what insurmountable challenges await the Deserted on those forbidding slopes?

"Tired yet?" Bernatelli calls over his shoulder. "Still think we should carry that dead weight around?"

"Yo, 'fit was you you be glad we done it, mufucka," says Shaneequio, without looking up from the dusty path. "'Fit was you we be all feedin' you grapes an shit, fuckin' fannin' yo ass with feathers an shit."

"I tell you to talk, pendejo?" Alejandra wheels around and smacks the gang counselor across the face. "I say you should open your fuckin' mouth?"

Shaneequio stares at his feet. "No ma'am."

Alejandra runs a fingernail under his chin, squeezes his jaw. "Then be a good boy and cállate la boca."

With a groan, Richard turns his head and vomits blood.

"I'm a winner," Gloria mutters at the back of the line, too low for the others to hear. "Yes, I am a winner."

"Armand," the producer says. "Por favor, ¿donde está Señor Armand?" The old woman bleats her incomprehensible reply—the same answer she's given every day since his return from the swamp. "¿Habla inglés?" he says. "¿Por favor, inglés?"

Outside, a blast of feedback screams into the night. Voices move through the clearing in twos and threes; animals cry overhead, alien noises from unfathomable sources. In the lulls a low, rhythmic roar can be heard: the ocean or the wind, some whispered expression of the island's malice. If he still had access, he could identify every sound. He could find out who was where, doing what to whom. But he has no access. He is blind as a mummy in a tomb, a ghost in his own machine.

"Do what you gotta do," Gloria said. "It's all the same to me." Would she really have done those things? In dark moments he's wondered what else she's capable of. He's even wondered what *really* happened to Candy, whether her fall was quite the accident it appeared to be. What happened to the sullen loner of the first five weeks, the object of his fascination? How could he have gotten Gloria so wrong?

"What kind of people are you?" she'd asked. And the truth is, he has no idea. He doesn't know who anyone is anymore—Gloria, Miley, Paco, even Armand. He's never really known any of them—thirteen years of transformations, televolutions, and he's never seen the first glimmer of truth. All his monitors and spycams, all his field logs and decision lists haven't touched it. Hundreds of players, thousands of techs and engineers, APs and VPs, locals working for pennies an hour, a wife who gave up her home for him, let him tear it down and rebuild it in the image of god-knows-who and then watched as he flew off to Chile and Mongolia—and all this time he's had it wrong. He's never known a fucking thing about any of them.

Sleepless at three AM, he scrolls through old emails, mostly unread—queries from journalists on six continents; invoices from gardeners and pool cleaners in L.A.; dozens of encouragements and threats from Boby, each more idiotic than the last. Frantic threads between the execs and the publicists, strategies for how to address the death of Stephanie Ann "Candy" Bright. A list of post-finale procedures sent by HR, the hundreds of steps necessary to break down the Facility and get everyone home.

"Be sure you take everything of value," the instructions say. "If you leave something important behind, you will probably never see it again."

Furiously deleting, approaching the Zen bliss of an empty inbox, he at last comes upon Patel's forgotten pitch, the sizable folder of documents, spreadsheets, and images taking up space on his private server. "I think you will agree it makes quite a good story," the director wrote, weeks ago now, referring to the draft proposal for a film about the history of the island. "I think people will be very interested to know what happened to this place and to these people. It's important."

He pages through the meticulously written treatment, the facilities list and pathetic attempt at a budget and laughable box office projections. He browses the appended anthropological studies, the reams of Ballard Corp.'s internal memos dealing with "the native question." He scans images of environmental devastation, photos of aboriginal villages taken before Ballard's arrival. He reads newspaper accounts, excerpts from executives' diaries, minutes of board meetings, directives from the UN High Commissioner for Refugees, shareholder reports, a letter of thanks to the CEO from President John F. Kennedy. Nowhere does he find evidence of marital infidelity. There is absolutely no mention of cross-dressing, or high-stakes poker, or kinky sex, or boob jobs. No one refers to the Lord Jesus Christ or speculates about extraterrestrials or sings show tunes or sues their neighbors over prodigal cats. No one crashes their own funeral or launches their baby in a hot-air balloon. Prada was a concept unknown to the island, as were *Grand Theft Auto*, metrosexuals, and fusion cuisine. The only tattoos in evidence are the ritual markings the aboriginals gave their children at puberty. What took place on this island was a sustained, premeditated atrocity: If he searched the files for a thousand years, he would encounter not a single thong.

The director's naiveté makes his stomach fall. No one will be "very interested." No one will be interested at all. Even Patel's process message breaks his heart: *Viewers will gain insight and empathy for those who have been harmed by our way of life.* The project is doomed, a nonstarter, he thinks, dragging everything into the recycling bin. Patel should stick with what he knows best, what audiences want: peeping Toms, shopping addictions, the inevitable failures of misplaced trust.

"You do good," his father used to say, when he came home from a sales trip, stoop-shouldered, smelling of desert highways. The producer never knew whether it was a question or a command. "You do good?" he'd say and the producer would roll his eyes. Once, they'd gone camping at the Grand Canyon, father and son; they'd sat on an outcropping somewhere along the South Rim. "All that's important is that you do good," his father said. "You try to make the world better than you found it." The producer, nineteen years old, on his way to college, considered throwing himself over the edge. His skin ached with resentment and sunburn. He was sure even the old man couldn't believe this crap.

Afternoon shade settled into the canyon, softening its lines and colors. The old man handed him a cold beer, magically acquired out of thin air. "When you walk into a room, are people happy to see you? That's how you know you did good: When you show up in someone's place of business, or their home, do they put down what they're doing and tell you they're glad you came?" But no one would tell the producer that now, even if he knew where anyone lived. And though he himself has many homes, they're all empty, not even a dog, or a goldfish, waiting for his return.

"You and me, Walter, ¿me entiendes? Gonna be you and me at that beach. You know that, right?" says Alejandra. Her voice is barely audible over the scraping of shoes on the path, the panting of breath. The camera follows close behind. Someone will subtitle this, the producer thinks. They'll splice in footage of the Deserted's first days on the island, the relative happiness of their first camp, all ten of them splashing in the ocean under clear skies.

"May the best man win," says Bernatelli, forging ahead.

Shot of Alejandra's face, the set of her jaw. "That's right," she nods. "May the best man win."

They set down Richard's litter and arrange themselves in the shade of an overhang. The producer clicks open the recycling bin and moves Patel's files back to the desktop. The least he can do is make some notes, he thinks, mark up the proposal. At least he can show Patel how to improve the general format, how to sex up a description enough to catch someone's eye. The idea might be going nowhere, but he can still help the guy out, right? Doesn't he owe the director that much?

No one speaks. No one looks at anyone else. The sun passes behind the mountains. Those with water do not offer it. If they did, no one would take it. The world is getting darker. The sound of drums pounding in the distance. Overhead, the sky wheels with vultures.

WEEK SEVEN

■

. . . previously

"Lord have mercy, you see the nips on the pharmacist? Hard as diamonds!" Jonesie crushes a cigarette butt into the glass ashtray on his console, lights another with his overcharged Zippo. "How'd you like to get your prescription filled by her, eh, Frank?"

"She's definitely pretty hot," the junior AP says, tentatively.

"Yeah," says Liam, the line producer, "and Bill Gates is pretty wealthy."

The control room swelters, thick with smoke and body odor. Early morning sun bakes the thatch roof; interns wilt against bamboo walls.

"Check out the derivatives trader," says Camera One. "You just know he wants Lydia to give him an injection!"

"Pharmacists don't give injections, dumbshit," says a logger.

"Come on, work with me here!"

"People, can we keep it down?" says the producer, waving his cup of rubber bands with one hand, covering his eyes with the other. On the program monitor, the Deserted have almost finished construction of the observation platform, eighty feet above the forest floor. Spikes driven into the trunk of a matumi tree make a precarious ladder; one by one, the players don harnesses, clip themselves to a safety rope, and climb.

"Looks like somebody's been taking extra spin classes," says Audio, as a UPS driver from San Diego starts the ascent, a close-up of his rear end filling the monitor.

"Camera Three," says Sandy, the director, and the shot changes, the climber seen now from above, peering up into the canopy with a determined grimace. "Wouldn't want you to get too excited," she tells Audio.

Jonesie stabs out another cigarette and sings, "*I love a man in a un-i-form . . .*"

"I'd stay away from that one," says Liam. "I hear a certain someone in Burbank has his eye on him."

Cut to a spectacular aerial shot of the Ouémé River, dazed and indolent in the morning light. Beyond the forest's edge, the near bank crowds with conical straw huts, cooking-fire smoke lying in lazy strata on the air. Ready the file footage of women washing clothes in the river, singing to the infants they carry in slings. Roll tape. Now a dizzying sweep back to the forest, zoom toward a cluster of tiny yellow dots in the highest tree, soon recognizable as the safety helmets worn by the seven remaining Deserted.

"Perfect, Camera One," Sandy says. "Beautiful stuff."

"I'd like to thank the Academy . . ." says Camera One.

"Seriously, though," says Audio. "No one's ass can be that firm. It's unnatural."

"Still on the UPS guy?" Jonesie says. "Listen to Liam. Armand's got dibs on that package."

"Nah, man," says the junior AP. "I thought Liam was talking about you." After a stunned second, the control room dissolves into snickers. Jonesie snatches him into a headlock.

"Not yet, Frank," Jonesie says, grinding his knuckles across the other AP's scalp. "You're still the new kid. Keep that in mind."

When Jonesie releases him, he falls back into his chair and rubs his head. "Can you stop calling me Frank?" he says. "It's Paco. Not that hard to remember."

"People, dammit, enough," says the producer, sprawled in his chair, still covering his eyes, his other hand sweeping the floor for his Bloody Mary. He got back from Cotonou less than an hour ago, whisked back at dawn in a military helicopter after an all-night party at the embassy. The dips and swerves as the chopper crossed the floodplain nearly undid him. "I have," he says, "a fucking hangover. I'd appreciate a little consideration."

"That's what she said!" says the chyron master.

"That's what your mom said!" says Camera Two.

"What does that even mean?" one intern asks another. Someone knocks on the control room door, but no one answers. On the P/V monitor, the UPS driver confers with the chiropractor about the edibility of crow eggs; on spycam three, a property manager fishes an energy bar from another player's pack; the still shop holds an image of a waterfall, frozen beneath the sweltering sky of southern Benin.

"Alright, we move to the river this afternoon," Jonesie tells the room. "Everyone has their assignments?" There are nods, grumbles, a couple of flipped birds. Jonesie turns to the producer and lowers his voice. "Someone's been calling you," he says, pointing to a stack of pink message slips. "You might think about calling her back."

The producer ignores him. "I think it was Jonesie's mom!" says Camera Two. "I'd definitely call her."

"Will you shut up?" Audio tells Camera Two, with a sympathetic glance at the producer. The knock comes again, more urgent. "The mom jokes are getting old."

"Right," Jonesie says, moving toward the door. "Save it for the poker table, okay? And what are *you* supposed to be, Stefan?" he says to someone outside. "Gone native, have you? Terrific."

On screen, the pharmacist gives the chiropractor a back rub. In the control room, two techs fight over a pair of pliers. The producer crushes a pink slip in his fist.

Jonesie squints at the person outside. "You're not Stefan," he says, and then the butt of a rifle smashes into his face, shattering the bridge of his nose and fracturing both orbital sockets with a sharp, metallic crack, knocking him backward to collapse like a shot horse on the control room floor.

Two gunshots slap the crew into shrieking panic. Four men in camouflage pants and sweat-stained gray tank tops crowd into the room. "Quiet now! *Silènce!*" shouts the one who fired the gun. "Everyone now on the floor." He fires another shot into the thatch as the others stride through the control room and shove the crew, one by one, to the floor amid the ringing echo. Camera Two puts up his hands and cries, "No problem, no problem!" and one of the men pistol-whips him across the jaw, shoves him face first to the floor, steps on the back of his neck, and points a rifle at his head. Audio presses herself into the space under her console, until a man drags her out by the hair, slaps her face, and drives his knee into her groin. The assailants are young men, some of them teenagers; all wear black caps with a green five-pointed star on the front. They move through the room in terse, practiced choreography, the clomp of their boots and the grunts of the crew filling the thick air. Chairs overturn, binders and cell phones clatter, the ashtray flips and sends up a stale cloud; one of the attackers stumbles over a trash bin and then kicks it viciously, sending a flurry of paper and plastic bottles across the floor. Someone moans, *"Oh my god . . . Oh my god . . ."* Someone else says, "Wait!" Two interns clutch each other in silent terror against the back wall while another starts to wheeze loudly. The leader of the assailants surveys the room and smiles, his face almost kind, his front teeth framed in dull metal. His eyes are bright, close together; his neck and collar covered in a dark rash or fungus; on one sinewy shoulder is tattooed the same green star they wear on their caps.

"Qui est le responsable?" he says in halting French. No one answers. Near his left foot, Jonesie's cigarette still smolders, a white vine of smoke trailing up into the thatch. "Who is in charge now?"

Across the room, Sandy screams, "Don't touch me!" as one of the attackers yanks her to her feet, thrusts his rifle in the small of her back, and moves her toward the door. "Now wait a minute—" says Liam, and the kid smashes a boot into the line producer's kneecap. Cameras One, Three, and Four lie parallel, face-down on the floor of the control room, hands laced behind their heads; the chyron master is slumped over his console. "It's cool, it's cool . . ." says Paco, lowering to his knees. "I'm cool, man. No gun, okay? No gun." Sandy clutches the doorframe as her attacker tries to drag her outside; she spits in his face and he clamps a hand around her neck, squeezing until she lets go of the door, shoving her outside where she falls choking to her knees. The gunman nearest Paco kicks him in the stomach. On the big screen, the Deserted make their way through a field of high rushes and head toward the village on the riverbank. When the washerwomen come on again, the leader of the group raises a pistol and shoots out all the monitors in a catastrophe of glass and spark and shattering noise.

"I ask you again, please," he says, strangely polite. "Who is in charge?"

No one answers. The man looks around the room, at the quivering crew, at Liam clutching his ruined knee in shock, at Jonesie unconscious on the floor before him, his face black with gore. He fires the pistol into Jonesie's abdomen. The senior AP's left arm jumps and thuds back to the floor.

"Tell me, please, who is in charge," he repeats.

"*Hey Jonesie, what the fuck?*" comes a hoarse voice from a walkie.

"Where do you want us? Get your thumb out of your ass and tell us where you want us!"

"I am," says the producer. "I'm in charge."

"Thank you. Will you come with me?" The leader's eyes flicker with light from the shot-out monitors. "General Godspeed would like to speak to you, please."

Head clanging, stomach loose and churning, the producer follows him out into the glare and chaos of the Facility. In the back of his mind, he wonders whether any of this is really happening, the slow disorientation of heat and hangover making it seem almost plausible that he's watching it from some invisible location or that he has seen it before—maybe last season? Across the broad, sepia plaza, jeeps criss-cross, revving their engines and honking their horns. Two or three men stand in the back of each jeep with rifles raised, all sporting black caps with green stars. Others swarm in and out of the editing huts, the mess hall, the cluster of tents on wood platforms that house most of the crew. Somewhere up ahead, he hears a familiar voice—Sandy's—screaming, but when he startles and tries to run after her the man kicks out his ankles and he falls heavily to the ground, his right shoulder taking his weight with a crunch.

"The general is waiting," the man says, leaning down to extend a courteous hand.

Everywhere are faces of people he knows. Everywhere, members of his crew are shoved at gunpoint, thrown across the hoods of jeeps, slapped hard, made to kneel blindfolded at the sides of buildings. Their cries resound through the Facility like the return of all the world's dead. "Qui est le responsable?" the man had asked, but the monstrousness of that word and all it implies won't sit still long enough for the producer to get a good look at it. His skin prickles; his shoulder throbs. Pointlessly, he looks for the military helicopter that brought him in, that must have shown the attackers their location—but the horizon is filled with dark clouds rolling in from the gulf. Already he can feel the humidity spiraling upward, the first quick gusts of a wind that will soon bend the trees. The leader throws an arm around his shoulder, as though they were old friends headed out for a beer, and they make their way through the confusion of jeeps toward an old brown Mercedes, immaculately polished, idling just inside the Facility's gates.

"Rain is coming," the leader says, sniffing at the clouds.

"What's happening here?" the producer says. Across the open space, soldiers pour gasoline over the canvas tents. The tin roof of the shower room flips off and crashes onto a golf cart. Next to the Sound hut, three men are clustered around someone on the ground; one hands his rifle to another and shoves his pants to his ankles. The door of Accounting is ajar, a pair of legs extending over the threshold. The producer's arm is numb to the wrist, his clavicle fractured, his fist frozen in a clench. The ringing in his ears is getting louder, overwhelming the shouts and the revving engines, but his vision is growing sharper, color and texture achieving painful saturation.

"Who are you?" he says. "What is happening?"

"The general will explain."

"What general? Do you understand what's happening here?" His breath is quick and shallow. "We're American citizens, do you know what you're doing?"

The man smiles his odd, boyish smile. "We know exactly who you are."

Week Four, midway point of a season that had seen unprecedented ratings, a spike in spot rates and product placement, advertisers clamoring around the network's sales execs like brokers on the floor of a stock exchange. This year's Deserted were an energetic bunch—they'd covered more territory than expected since having been shipwrecked in the Bight of Benin twenty-three days ago, churning out some terrific internecine conflict and a musical chairs of showmance along the way. The crew had been working extremely well, an almost preconscious cooperation that made the producer's job all the easier. Paco seemed to have finally settled in, and Jonesie, despite the hazing, had confided that he'd never seen someone so obviously destined to have his own show. This, plus the occasional field trip to Cotonou, where the producer had been introduced to a sexually gifted assistant to the French consul who was an ardent fan of the show, had made preproduction and the first three weeks a virtual cakewalk, and he sometimes lost sight of the fact of his own control, his responsibility, swept along in the momentum of events that seemed almost to produce themselves. All the while, scouts from the Niger Delta People's Army had been conducting surveillance on the Facility, the movements of the crew, the arrival of cargo, the comings and goings of helicopters from Cotonou. There had been reports of new exploration by Western oil corporations in the marshlands of southern Benin, continued discussion among regional plutocrats about a pipeline through Benin and Togo and Ghana to a sea terminal in Côte d'Ivoire where tankers could glut themselves on African resources to power the cars and large-screen televisions and megasupermarkets and general bacchanalia of American and European life, at the expense of the continued oppression, butchery, and impoverishment of the long-suffering Ogoni and Ijaw people who lived on the land but never saw one penny of the revenue. The NDPA, which until now had consisted of loosely affiliated bands spread through the villages and old forests of western Nigeria, responsible only for a series of shrill press releases and the destruction of a dozen or so abandoned military vehicles, did not know quite what to make of the installation just over the border in Benin—which seemed to lack the heavy machinery, beetling engineers, and ostentatious security detail of, say, Shell's flow stations in the delta—but that there was some connection to the oil thieves

and murderers who had turned their homes into hells of exploita-
tion and violence was never in question. Seeing an easy target, they
set up a staging area and General Godspeed convened his regional
commanders, who chose the date. With this mission, they would
send a simple message: *Stop what you are doing.* The people would
not tolerate an expansion of the abuse, an acceleration of the deg-
radation of their way of life; henceforth they would rise up against
foreign rapacity and do what was necessary to preserve their land,
their resources, and their dignity. The operation would be swift and
merciless, its meaning clear. Foreign corporations would reconsider
this latest outrage, if only because the risk to their reputations,
and their balance sheets, was too great. Having sucked as much
lifeblood from the earth as they could afford to suck, they would
dismantle their wells and their off-shore platforms and slink off like
cowards in the night in search of more easily and safely oppressed
populations, perhaps somewhere in Asia, and the Nigerian people,
along with their brothers and sisters in Benin, would be restored to
ultimate control over their own lives.

By the end of the day, there would be five dead crew members,
all shot at close range, four of whom had multiple bones broken and
one of whom—a twenty-four-year-old grip from Van Nuys—was
raped by three NDPA soldiers, her breasts carved from her body, her
throat slit, left sprawled on a table in the mess to die. There would
be dozens of injuries, from broken ribs to third-degree burns to stab
wounds in the face, back, breasts, and groin. Once the military, the
Red Cross, and officials from the U.S. State department finally arrived
after nightfall, it would take the better part of a day to find everyone,
some of the crew having fled into the forest or barricaded themselves
inside smaller buildings and prayed no one set them on fire. Six crew
members, including Sandy Beers, would be unaccounted for, until a
fax would arrive in the embassy in Lagos demanding the immediate
expulsion of all foreign petroleum companies and their subsidiaries

from West Africa; negotiations would last several weeks, at the end of which five of the hostages would be released, the sixth, an accountant from Ventura, having died of a massive seizure because he did not have his epilepsy medication. After nearly forty-eight panic-stricken hours in which they received no instructions from the Facility, the field teams and the Deserted would once again proceed north along the muddy, imperturbable Ouémé, having been told that a fire briefly knocked out communications but that all was now well, and the show would continue as planned. When, after the finale, they would learn the truth of what happened, six players would file a multimillion-dollar suit against the network for negligence and mental anguish. The suit would be settled out of court for an undisclosed sum, an agreement reached by all parties never to speak of the unfortunate incident again.

As he approached the general's Mercedes, the producer, of course, knew none of this. He knew only that the wind was kicking up—a wet, muscular wind from the south, after months of the bone-dry Harmattan—and that he could no longer hear the screams of his crew. He could see nothing but the oddly serene face of the man who guided him, and the black smoke heaving up from the thatch roof of the control room. He thought briefly of the cigarette that had fallen from Jonesie's fingers. He thought of the rooftop bar in Kathmandu where he and Jonesie and Paco had drained a bottle of scotch after last season's finale. He thought of the French woman in Cotonou, who'd said flirtatiously over a glass of Shiraz when they'd first met, "So you are the one who sets it all in motion. You are the invisible hand." His eyes burned and his sinuses were plugged and swollen; his shoulder ached unbearably and his right arm was both cold and hot, almost immovable; and as they stopped before the car and a tinted back window slowly lowered, he unclenched his fist with searing pain and looked down to find, inexplicably, a crumpled pink message slip in his hand.

"You will tell them," said the man inside the car. The producer had the impression of a narrow face, light-skinned and bespectacled, of a voice that was learned but only reluctantly demanding. The general did not wear a hat. "You will tell them what happened here. That it is the inevitable result of your own greed and disrespect. No one is immune. No one is unaccountable. You will tell them you have brought this upon yourselves."

The producer found himself shivering. When he said nothing, the man at his side put a hand on his holster. "Answer the general," he said.

"No," said the general. His eyes did not leave the producer. "He will tell them." He stared at the producer a moment longer as the rainclouds' heavy shadow swept across the Facility and the wind, all at once, died out.

"What is in your hand?" the general said. When he had deliberately unfolded and smoothed the pink message slip, the general examined it with great solemnity and handed it back. "You should call your wife," he said. Someone inside the car laughed, but the general only turned his gaze away and the tinted window came up again and showed to the producer a pale and insubstantial version of himself.

"Go now," said the man with the gun.

But for several long minutes, the producer went nowhere. Behind him, gunshots alternated with the clamor of structures collapsing. Six crew members, tied at the wrists and ankles, were tossed into the backs of jeeps, which sped off toward the gate. Two soldiers ushered Paco and the others out of the control room but left Jonesie's body to burn. The producer saw none of it. He heard nothing, even when the Mercedes' engine started and the car turned smartly and headed back out onto the road and the soldier who had been guarding him, for no apparent reason, saluted him and then turned back to gather his men, to declare the operation a total success and orchestrate their withdrawal, and left him standing at the edge of his devastated Facility, face turned up to a motionless sky, to the dark and excruciating swelling that any moment now would burst open upon them all and drown them in the waters of a rainy season that was just beginning.

Tonight, after seven long weeks, the struggle, the danger, the agony, comes to an end. Forty-four days they've fought their way across brutal terrain, endured extreme weather, wild animals, the fury of the island's gods. Forty-four days—they've crossed raging rivers, navigated a burning labyrinth, suffered crippling hunger and thirst in the desolate badlands. Alliances formed and broken, trust betrayed, friends lost forever. In the end, they've learned the hardest lesson of all: You can only rely on yourself.

Once there were ten. Now, four remain. Who will be the last one standing? Sergeant Walter Bernatelli, who's excelled in every test of skill and athleticism? Alejandra Ruiz, whose grit and determination have made her an audience favorite? Shaneequio Jones, the dark horse, whose life in the gangs of L.A. couldn't prepare him for the island's warfare? Or Gloria Hamm, strong but silent, waiting all these weeks for her chance?

Everything comes down to these last ordeals. Who will be crowned Lord of the Island?

Not even the producer knows.

"What's with the fucking band?" he says. "Are they going to wear the tunics or not?" He's been awake since three, since the guards unlocked his trailer and escorted him to the command center. The latest snafu: Coldplay doesn't like what Wardrobe came up with. His attitude: Too bad for Coldplay. "Anyone figure out the Porta-John issue?"

The Deserted have arrived at the Wall of Doom, a towering climb up a sheer rock face. Should they manage to scale it—and they will—they'll arrive, at last, at the cave, where the producer will see his vision made real. Then: the furious race to Paradise Beach, the gala celebration, slaughter of goats, Coldplay, etc.

The crew bustles; the producer squirms. The guards had bound him to the chair with bungee cords, coaxial cables; only Miley's intercession kept the gag out of his mouth. "Someone want to tell me why there's a condom on the drum riser?" he says.

Behind him, a female intern gasps. "Sorry, sir," mutters a kid from Electrical.

"What kind of show you running here, Lobo?" the producer says. Paco, busy going over assignments with Taylette, waves him off. "You think this is Week Two? Better get on the stick."

"I think the math teacher got on the stick last night!" says Camera One. Miley flashes him a radioactive glare. He takes a new-found interest in his scopes.

"Details, Paco. You wanted your own show, better pay attention to the details." The senior AP walks back to check with the story assistants; the producer calls after him, but can't turn around. "Not as easy as it looks, is it?" he says. "It's not just about power, Paco. Responsibility! Everyone's counting on you. What are you going to do?"

The command center is tightly clenched, humming with anxiety. They've done live segments before, but never a finale—it's the ulti-mate test of the crew's mettle, an ordeal all its own. To make things worse, a rival network has put up its own special programming: Candy Bright's funeral procession through the streets of Denver, with expected attendance north of 100,000.

"This is our Super Bowl, dudes. Don't eff it up," Boby told the crew in a video pep talk, shown on every screen in the Facility. "Go win one for the Bobster."

From the Audio Empire, a passionate cry: "¡Ándale, mamita!" Alejandra has pulled ahead on the Wall of Doom, raising herself in painstaking, tendon-stretching increments. Bernatelli and Shane-equio climb in parallel far below. Gloria, tangled in her harness, has barely gotten off the ground.

"Ready Five, then One," Patel says. "Okay, go Five." A distance shot of the wall, the players just tiny growths on the mountain's vast, forbidding face.

"Best you can do?" the producer says.

"What would you recommend?" the director asks coolly.

The producer kicks his heels against the base of the chair. Pleased with this petulance, he does it again. "Ask the señor back there. It's not my call."

"Helmet-cam," Paco calls out. The shot changes to a shaky close-up, Bernatelli's sweat-sheened forearms filling the screen, muscles dancing like piano wire as he grips a rough outcropping. When he looks up, the wall's daunting height canting into the sky, Alejan-dra's ass is a dozen meters above.

"That's the ticket!" says Camera One.

"Beautiful, Lobo," says the chyron master. "You're the best."

Bernatelli is breathing hard. His strained voice fills the room. *"Take her down . . . Let's go, Walter, get up there . . . You gonna let a girl beat you?"*

"They put on the tunics or they don't get paid," the producer says. "You hear me, Paco?"

"Are you okay?" says Miley. She crouches by the chair, puts a hand on his shoulder. In answer, he lunges halfheartedly against the cables. His cup of rubber bands totters off the armrest and spills onto the floor mats.

"You think we could turn up the air?" he says. Two interns scramble for the climate control. "Is this fucking Calcutta? Jesus Christ, Lobo, you trying to lose weight?"

"You need anything?" Miley says. "Can I make you more comfortable?"

"*Ten hut!*" Bernatelli croaks. "*Get up that wall, soldier!*" Around the room, a volley of responses: "Ten hut! Grab that ass, soldier!" "Bite me, soldier!" "Get it up, Sarge!"

"Comfortable?" He stares at the scar under Miley's ear: the mark of the betrayer. "I'll take a double scotch, neat," he says. "And how about some shiatsu?"

Miley sucks her teeth. "No one's happy about this."

Behind him Paco says, "Ten minutes, people! Time to get busy. We got ten minutes tops before they're in the cave."

The producer nods toward the senior AP. "He seems pretty happy about it."

"Look, I got you back in," she says. "That's the best I could do."

"Just remember our deal."

The knock on the trailer door had roused him from a dream in which the Deserted, one by one, reached down his throat and pulled out fistfuls of squirming viscera. Thirteen seasons of them—he'd lain on a gurney in an operating room and the Deserted lined up down the hall. "Dr. Lecter," said the chyron master, when the guards trussed him into the chair, "would you like some fava beans with your liver?" Techs snickered behind their hands; interns clung to the back wall, awestruck by his captivity.

Curtain-up was the goodbye to Richard, whom the other players left in a stand of cypress trees, the parting shot an award-worthy handheld of the hairdresser in his litter, not long for this world, giving his companions a final thumbs-up. The whole room gaped at the pathos, the simple genius of it. A group email from Boby came seconds later, composed entirely of emoticons.

"Okay, Weather," Paco says into his walkie. "Time to make it interesting."

Gusting winds are raised, the island's breath turning against the four trespassers. The Deserted flatten themselves against the Wall of Doom as storm clouds race across the sky. Soon there will be hail. As the wind howls through the slot, Shaneequio loses his chalk bag and, lunging recklessly, almost loses the game.

"What's happening in Denver?" the producer asks. No one answers. "Hello? Anyone remember me?"

A moment of stillness. Shot of a dusty cliff edge, the old forest far below. In the distance the tranquil ocean. A perfect three-second interval, until: chalky fingers clutch at the dirt, now a forearm, now the top of a head . . .

Alejandra has conquered the Wall of Doom!

Cue "The Ride of the Valkyries."

Cheers fill the control room.

"Keep it under control, people," says Paco. "Still a lot of work to do."

"That's what she said!" says Camera One.

"Last chance, Lobo," says the chyron master. "Wet T-shirt contest in the cave?"

"Hey!" the producer says. "Want to work cable-access for the rest of your life?"

The chyron master and Camera One exchange looks of mock terror, then high fives. Alejandra peers over the edge of the cliff and lets a silky line of saliva string down toward Bernatelli's face.

"Do you remember me?" his wife said that day by the pool. "Do you know who I am?" He'd watched the hummingbirds, sipped his mojito. He could feel her staring, but he would not turn around. "Hello? Do you remember marrying me?"

Now three of the Deserted stand atop the wind-swept escarpment—battered, bloody, leaning on their knees. "Patel," the producer says, as Gloria heaves a heavy leg over the top of the cliff. "I want to talk to you later, Patel. I want to talk about that movie. I read your stuff. Pretty interesting."

Patel turns with a surprised smile. "You really think so?" he says.

"Needs a lot of work. But it might have a shot. Be an uphill battle, though, you know that."

"Here we go!" says Taylette, as the Deserted gather at the entrance to the cave. Gloria squats panting, face and arms streaked with grime, while the others strain to move the giant boulder that has been placed there, the forbidding stone marked with the sign of the Sky Mother, Xim.

I'm a winner, Gloria had said. *I'm the real thing.* But which *I* did she mean? The silent Gloria, who'd opted out for five weeks, or the one who'd offered her body as a bribe, a sacrifice? He's gone over hours of footage, read her casting file forwards and backwards, but he still doesn't know who she really is.

Miley, signing off on a runner's clipboard, returns to crouch at his side. "Listen. There's something I need to tell you."

The best he's come up with is that they were both roles, both fakeries. Gloria had kept her true self hidden, chosen one lie and then, when it proved ineffective, switched to another. It was all strategy, he's decided. They've never seen the real Gloria. She's probably never set foot on this island.

"There've been some changes," Miley says. "I just want you to hear it from me."

But then, late last night, an even more terrifying thought: What if there was no real Gloria? What if there were only more roles?

"Let me guess: It never happened, the thing with Boby," he tells Miley. "You were lying to me, back in the bunker. See? I get it."

She frowns. "It's my job to do what's best for you, you understand? Even when it's not what you think you want. That's why I was hired: to protect you. To watch your back. I want you to remember that, okay?"

"You wanted something from me, so you played on my sympathy. Made me think I owed you," he says. "It was strategy. You'd never go that far. You're not like the rest of these people. Right?" On the monitor, Alejandra yanks Gloria by the hair; Shaneequio delivers a vicious head-butt to Bernatelli. "Miley?"

Miley pulls at a thread on her shirt. "That doesn't matter anymore."

"It does matter."

"No, it doesn't," she says. "I told you it happened. So it happened."

"But I'm asking you for the truth."

The stone rolls away, the dark cave beckons. Miley raises her eyes. "The truth," she says, disgusted. "What do you want it to be? I told you a story. I can't untell it. Obviously I wanted you to believe it."

"But—"

"The story *is* the truth. Don't you know that by now? Once it's told, once you've seen it in your mind, you can't unsee it. That's televolution. That's what we do here. Facts, history—who cares?"

"But is it true?"

She stares at him, and a sad smile blooms across her mouth. For a second she seems like a different person—uncertain, someone who doesn't fit so effortlessly into the world. Someone who might need him.

"It is now," she says. She touches his cheek. "Don't drive yourself crazy. Let's just write a good ending."

Behind her, heads bowed, the Deserted file into the Cave of Truth.

"One at a time!" he says. Then, to Miley, "They're supposed to go one at a time."

She looks away. "Just try to relax," she says.

The first thing he notices is the lack of guano. Where six weeks ago he'd found a slippery expanse of putrid slime, the cave is dry and immaculately swept, the stone smooth, almost polished. The bats have been exterminated. These decisions were made at the highest level. Lighting has done a commendable job on short notice: a warm amber glow from sconces set into the walls, an optimal shadow complexity, a nice flicker frequency despite the underwriters' prohibition on open flames. Iron rings have been mounted at regular intervals, streaked with a brownish film that may be rust or blood.

"I said *no changes*," the producer says. "Did you people read the blocking? Did you even look at the ground plan?"

Back at her console, Miley closes her eyes. Someone has tuned a monitor to the rival network. The streets of Denver throng with mourners. The human sea parts slowly, making way for a coffin festooned with flowers.

"I'm off," says Paco. "Gotta execute some goats. I'll give a shout from the beach."

"Get your ass back here!" says the producer. "What did you do to my cave?"

"Okay, you fucking maricones, bring it on!" Alejandra shouts into the cave's recesses. She turns to the camera, raises her middle finger. "Fuck you, too," she says. "May the best *woman* win." Shane-equio tries to free himself by gnawing at his leash. Bernatelli takes off his shirt. Gloria, silent and wary, presses her back to the wall.

The producer jerks from side to side. He clutches the armrests until the cords raise welts on his arms as men in black ski masks swarm into the cave, immobilizing the Deserted, lashing them to the iron rings, circling the room with snarling Rottweilers.

"Tell the truth!" the men shout. They slap the Deserted across their faces. "Tell the truth, you pieces of shit!"

"This is not what I wanted," the producer says. "What are you people doing?"

From behind him, Paco's voice: "We're winning. We're getting back on top."

The men shove filthy rags into the Deserted's mouths, smack their heads, kick their ribs. They are careful not to leave marks. They brandish a live electrical cable. The dogs slaver and menace. These procedures were approved at the highest level. We have documents from Legal. We have waivers from the underwriters.

"You idiot," the producer says. "This isn't what we set out to do."

"Ain't it, though?" Paco says.

"I said a dark room. I said they come alone. Just them and the cave, the truth of their own hearts." He can hear the silliness of it, the flimsiness, but he doesn't care. "We had a chance to do something real. I told you it wasn't about ratings. It wasn't supposed to be violent or sensational." With a mighty wrench, he half-turns to face his former assistant. "It was supposed to be about love."

The room is silent but for the sound of blows through the speakers. Finally Paco spits out a laugh that's less cruel than amused, as though a toddler just used a dirty word and hadn't the slightest idea of its meaning.

"Dreamin', Boss," he says. With a nod to Miley, he turns for the door.

"Paco!" he says. "Get the fuck back here, Paco! You owe me. You'd still be shoveling elephant shit if it weren't for me, you ungrateful S.O.B." On the console, he spots the battered copy of *Loving God with All Your Mind*. "You forgot your little book, Paco!"

Paco turns in the doorway, a shadow speaking out of the glare. "You can have it, boss. You should check it out. It's weird," he says. "It's almost like you coulda wrote it."

Now, on the line monitor, the men yank the rags from the Deserted's mouths. "Tell us the truth!"

Shaneequio's head lolls. Alejandra appears to be unconscious. "*Semper fi*," Bernatelli gasps. "I'm a Marine. Stand down!" A deep rumble rises from the mountain's heart, a fine shower of grit falling from the roof.

"Take it easy, Audio," Taylette says.

"I'm cool," says Audio.

"Yeah, you're cool," says Miley. "Remember Mongolia?"

"Only the truth can get you out of here," says one of the masked men.

One by one, the Deserted are released from the iron rings, their wrists bound behind them with ropes that stretch to the ceiling. When the ropes go taut their arms jerk horribly, inverting behind their backs and over their heads until their shoulder joints bulge. Their toes lift several inches off the ground.

"That's some medieval shit right there," says Camera Two.

"Oh, please," says Taylette. "Palestinian hanging? We used to do this back in high school."

In Denver, mourners swarm around Candy's coffin, bringing the procession to a standstill. The multitudes beat their breasts, rend their garments.

"Where are you?" his wife had said. "Can you tell me?" She'd said it so many times: on the phone, on the fax machine, on his BlackBerry. He was in Morocco. He was in Greenland. Some new country whose name ended with -stan. Or, he was in his own back-yard, his closed eyes swimming red in the afternoon heat.

"Do you know who I am?" she'd said, her voice distant, disem-bodied. He did know. He did remember marrying her. That wasn't the problem. But when he remembered it, he saw both of them. He didn't see her as he'd seen her then, standing so close, the errant blob of mascara at the corner of one eye. He didn't feel her hand shaking in his as they said the vows. Instead, he saw them both from a near distance, their backs stiff like figures atop a wedding cake, saw the panorama of the Pacific Ocean beyond them, a per-fectly framed scene he had never actually experienced. He saw them as though he were in the audience.

"Ready Camera One," Patel says quietly. "Take one."

Now the Deserted are lowered to the floor, left to lie in broken, semi-conscious agony, Rottweilers growling over them. A gurney is wheeled to the center of the cave. More grit showers from above, the image unsteady, shaken by unimaginable forces.

"Please stop," the producer says, as they cut off the Deserted's clothing with shears. Miley won't meet his eyes. "Please, you don't know what you're doing."

"Holy shit! Anyone watching the blogs?" says Taylette.

An intern says, "You can't believe this spike in text messages!"

Shaneequio, naked except for blue bikini briefs, is thrown onto the gurney, his legs and arms restrained, a thin cloth stretched tight over his nose and mouth. "Pulse up to 140," says a tech. Everyone is focused on the monitors, everyone sensing triumph. In a screening room in Burbank, Boby reaches for his secretary's hand.

A bucket is brought from the back of the cave. The interrogators raise it over Shaneequio's face and water slowly spatters onto the cloth. The water fills his mouth and his nasal passages, pushes into his throat like a tight, implacable fist.

"One-sixty!" cries the tech.

"Miley," whispers the producer.

There are terrible gurgling noises. Shaneequio's head explodes with panic, with white fire. His chest rises against the restraints; his back smashes and recoils against the stainless steel; his bound ankles start to bleed. There was considerable discussion about this particular procedure. In the end, a determination was made.

"I'm a winner," says Gloria. One of the masked men punches her in the stomach.

"Email is like thirty-to-one favorable!" an intern whispers.

"I told you," says the chyron master. "I told you we do the gang-banger first."

The producer slumps against the bungee cords. "Miley, we had a deal."

Shaneequio's body jumps and spasms. His eyes bulge; his lungs stretch and burn. He is close to cardiac arrest. Our doctors are monitoring the situation. "The truth!" shout the interrogators. One of them drives an elbow into the drowning man's gut. "Tell the truth and we'll let you go."

"Listen to this," Taylette says, reading from her iPad. "'These pampered movie stars had it coming. They tortured me for seven weeks. Now it's their turn!'"

"Sounds like we found our promo copy," says an editor.

"This isn't what I meant," the producer groans. "It was supposed to be about love."

"You will tell them," said General Godspeed. But he never did. "You have brought it on yourself," said the general. But it was worse than that: He'd brought it on *them*—the players, the crew, everyone he'd ever touched. They'd left Stan on a skiff in the empty ocean. Simon was hurled into a raging river. Candy fell into the labyrinth and died without knowing it. Richard, Clarice, the dozens who came before them—all cast aside, all deserted. Jonesie, dead in an African hut. His wife, left in a house she couldn't recognize, pregnant with a child she'd never deliver. Paco was right. The show was his creation. In the end, he was *le responsable*.

"I'm sorry," he says, but no one is listening.

One by one, the Deserted are strapped to the gurney, drowned and resuscitated repeatedly, brought to the edge of death and then thrown to the floor to shiver and black out. The control room cheers them on. Techs exchange five-dollar bills; interns clutch one another and sob. In Burbank, the lawyers sign off on documents. The suits put in calls to their travel agents.

"We had a deal, Miley," he groans. "You said you believed in me. How could you let Paco do this?"

Alejandra crawls to Shaneequio and starts mouth to mouth. The interrogators sponge blood and feces off the gurney.

"Paco didn't do anything," she says. Miley turns to him with a raised chin. "He did what he was told."

Candy's coffin has arrived at the gravesite. Mo'nique sings the first lines of "Amazing Grace."

"Boby?" the producer whispers.

Miley shakes her head. "I promised to look out for you. I'm sorry. I really am."

The masked men have disappeared. Coughing and groaning, the Deserted shamble to the mouth of the cave, where they discover final instructions etched into the walls. The crude drawings of hunters, of animals, of the island's topography, have been laser-enhanced, augmented with maps and diagrams. A mural has been commissioned depicting Paradise Beach, its legend written in a calligraphy of blood: *The Promist Land*.

"It was the only way," Miley says.

The Deserted scrawl their Last Testaments on parchment, race outside to assemble parachutes from scraps of animal hide. The speakers roar with subterranean thunder. On four input monitors, the luau is about to begin: party boats hovering off the north shore, the beach presided over by the stage, video screens, a golden banner stretched across the finish line, one corner loose and flapping in the wind so it reads I AM THE LORD O.

The mountain shudders; a broad dagger of stone calves from a nearby slope. The four players clasp one another's shoulders, solemnly recalling what they've been through together, acknowledging the bond that has formed between them—stronger than friendship, something no one else will ever understand.

Gloria is the first to speak. "It's been real," she says, then flings herself off the cliff.

The producer hiccups once and starts to cry.

"Fuck," Miley says.

As he watches her fall through the air—in close-up, in wide

angle, in a staccato, looping slo-mo—a long whine leaks from his throat. He hangs his head, held to the chair only by the coaxials, and weeps uncontrollably. His nose starts to run. Miley snaps orders, redirects everyone's attention; she comes to his side and rubs the back of his neck.

"It's okay," she says.

Sobs crash through him. He tries Ujayyi breathing, tries looking through his third eye. But Gloria is still falling. There's no special effect that can stop it, no trickery or editing that can keep her from the bottom. It's too late for intervention, for anything but the cruel work of gravity. He's responsible for all of it. Responsible and absolutely impotent.

"It's okay," Miley says. "See? The parachute worked."

Alejandra plummets missile-like after Gloria, waiting until the last instant to pull her cord. Shaneequio's parachute fails to open— roll the tape of Bernatelli using a nail file on his ripcord. The Dash to Paradise is on; the last three players stumble and sprint through the jungle, skirt tar pits, dodge fallen trees and striking cobras, run through a menacing gauntlet that the producer designed trunk by fern by stone. Techs fall to their knees, cheering on their favorites; Audio is beside himself trying to control levels; Taylette screams into her headset to get a medical team out to Shaneequio.

Miley presses the producer's head to her chest. "It's okay."

The island is loath to let them escape. Roots suddenly protrude; vines stretch tight as garrotes; quicksand yawns where once there was solid ground. The computer runs it all at random, the program adapted from military flight-combat simulators, run through a server farm even Boby doesn't know about. When a poison dart barely misses Gloria, the producer is wracked by a spasm of wet coughs.

"I'm sorry," he stammers, though he knows it's too late for that, too. "I'm sorry."

Miley closes her eyes. She touches her jaw and says, "I forgive you."

Then she reaches behind him and undoes the cables, works her hands between his body and the cushions to untie his arms. When all the cords have fallen to the floor, she turns back to the monitors, where Gloria has a slim lead on Bernatelli. The race is almost over, Paradise Beach and the finish line minutes away.

"It's your show," Miley says.

Tentatively, he slides out of the chair. Miley's seat is empty, her computer logged in and awaiting commands. Gloria vaults a fallen tree, widening her lead. Her eyes are ablaze with determination, her hair wild, her face flushed. She's almost beautiful.

"What are you waiting for?" Miley says.

It was neither an act, nor was it genuine, he thinks. Those categories no longer make sense. Maybe Gloria would have done those things and maybe she wouldn't—but none of it has any bearing on who she really is. Maybe she killed Candy, maybe not. Maybe she isn't even a dental hygienist—what does it matter? When the show is over, she'll be someone else, no more related to the woman on the island than a butterfly is related to a beefworm. The truth is that she's no one at all, reality's ultimate extension, its apotheosis: something so minutely manipulated it's indistinguishable from a real person.

She's a monster, he thinks. Of course she deserves to win.

Bagpipes blare as Candy's coffin is lowered into the ground.

The players have neared the edge of the forest.

"You're the producer," Miley says. "The show's whatever you want it to be."

"I'm going now," his wife had said. But she stood there for a long time first.

How many alternate endings has he imagined? How many sequels?

With a savage cry Bernatelli knocks Alejandra to the ground, then closes fast on Gloria. Coldplay is taking the stage. They're wearing the tunics. The horizon is crowded with helicopters, smudged with smoke from booming cannons. As Paco's voice spits from a walkie, Bernatelli, covered head to foot in tar, swings on a vine and kicks Gloria hard between the shoulders.

"Cunt," he says, tripping over her, crawling the last yards to the sand.

The producer clutches the mouse, one hand poised over the keyboard. The command center howls like a wind tunnel, everyone shouting, pumping their fists. With one command he could override the algorithms, drop Bernatelli into a bottomless well. He could bring down lightning, smite that son of a bitch with the click of a mouse.

A helicopter shot of the glittering white beach, three dark specks converging on the finish line. Patel shouts into his headset and Coldplay rips into their first number, drums pounding from every speaker, guitars ringing out.

The producer squeezes the mouse so hard his torso shakes. He's wailing like a lunatic, the players only seconds away, when a flickering image distracts him—out of the corner of his eye he sees the strangest thing: a woman all in white, standing alone at the side of a grave. As the producer hesitates, she bows her head and tosses a handful of dirt over the coffin.

"Hiroko?" he says.

That's when the command center falls silent.

The cheering breaks off; the walkies go dead. Even the music stops, the last chords clattering in on themselves, a short whine of feedback and the click of drumsticks falling to the stage.

"Oh, my lord," Taylette says.

Gloria, Bernatelli, and Alejandra have pulled up short, panting side by side a dozen yards from the finish line. The members of Coldplay stare at one another in confusion. Patel and the chyron master and all the cameras shake their heads as though to clear a dream, everyone onscreen and off staring at a dark shape emerging from the jungle.

"Dear god," someone says.

In pale sunlight, the figure moves haltingly, jerking forward and swaying across the sand. Cameras pan and zoom, racking in and out of focus. Groans fill the command center. The producer reaches into his pocket for his favorite stone, but it's at the bottom of the swamp. In a daze, Miley sinks to the edge of the chair.

Small and misshapen, the figure lurches toward them, one ashy brown leg stiff as a log, blood-streaked and covered with boils; the other scarred and twisted, bent implausibly, angling to a blunt, toeless foot which she drives into the sand to anchor her weight and drag her other leg forward.

Someone holds a phone to the producer's ear. *"You're finished, dude,"* comes Boby's tinny voice. *"This is it, shitbag, you're done!"*

Her face looks as though a clumsy sculptor scraped it from the thin, speckled flesh of her neck: chinless and flat, her nose a bony hummock merged with a cleft lip. One of her eyes is worm-colored, wet; the other looks straight into the camera. In her arms she holds a tiny, black bundle: the producer can make out a wizened scalp, a lumped face with no eyes, a small mouth frozen in a cry. Trails of dry, crusted milk streak the woman's belly. What first appeared to be a ribbon or strip of hide is an umbilical cord, swinging lightly as she walks.

"Who on earth . . ." Patel says, but leaves off, knowing exactly who, knowing, as does everyone in the room, as does everyone in Burbank, every person watching from home, what she is—this hideous, miserable creature, this stark figure of accusation, of fear, of shame, condensation of all the pointless loathing and pain the island has coughed out of its black and angry soul.

And you: You know her, too.

Don't you?

The Deserted kneel in the sand, frozen by the sight of her. When she holds out her bundle, Bernatelli turns and retches. Alejandra faces the nearest camera in horror. Gloria hugs herself, teeth chattering, but doesn't look away.

No one breathes. The wind and the waves have stilled.

"Camera Two," Patel whispers. "Now, please." But the shot doesn't change.

When Gloria reaches for the bundle, the woman raises her face to the tropical sky and lets out a shrill, inhuman cry. The sound races across the beach, carries back into the forest, across the badlands and the ice flats, the Mangrove Swamp and the Volcanic Labyrinth that still bubbles with manmade heat. It speeds through canyons and climbs sheer rock faces, penetrates mountain passes and mine shafts and all the island's secret places. It is as though her scream can be heard in the command center itself—not through cables and receivers but in the pure waveforms of its original sound. It spikes every meter, trips every alarm. The crew doubles over and covers their ears—all but the producer, whose every sinew, every blood cell cries out in sympathy, his body clutched by grief, dancing rigid as an electrocution, until the woman on the beach closes her horrible mouth and he falls back in stunned relief.

Into Gloria's arms she relinquishes her dead child.

Bernatelli spits in the sand and says something the mics don't pick up. A perfect shot of Alejandra, smashing his skull with a plank.

The members of Coldplay turn off their amplifiers and quietly leave the stage.

Miley squeezes the producer's hand. Her eyes shine with something like pride.

Shaneequio, who has dragged himself to the beach—broken ribs, broken ankle, and all—collapses into Alejandra's arms.

The producer watches all of them, shivering with an elation he can't understand.

Dancers take off their grass skirts. Helicopters recede into the sky. Paco spares the lives of the last four goats.

The game is over. All cameras go cold.

There will be no Lord of the Island.

It's time for you to go home.

The Off-Season

■

In 1952, Ballard Metals Corp. promised the island's inhabitants a new home on Vanuatu, a school for their children, and a tribal development endowment they had no intention of funding. Of the 1,400 known inhabitants, nearly all relocated, but a few dozen stayed, huddling in the rainforest after their villages were razed, staging occasional forays into the company compound. The caves where their gods lived were flooded or dynamited; their fields were turned into slurry ponds that gleamed with oily trailings in the tropical sun. Over the years several natives were shot trying to enter the mines, or snatching clothing from laundry bins, or begging food too close to the company pier; one teenager was lynched for raping an engineer's wife. Ballard left the island in 1999. The native population had dwindled to a handful, chronically malnourished, riddled with rare tumors and hereditary defects. The rivers and aquifers bubbled with arsenic, lead, cyanide; the caves breathed poison. Most of the women were barren, the few live offspring deformed, mentally retarded, genetically ruined. They knew nothing of gods. They had no names and no language and so could not name their isolation. They existed briefly and painfully for an average of twenty-two years and then they died unnoticed. When, years later, the first helicopter landed on the beach, emblazoned with a colorful logo, they could not even articulate the hope that they were saved.

Here is how Miley got her scar. As an awkward, unhappy teenager, she found comfort volunteering at an animal shelter. After a year there she brought home a stray, a tenacious mutt scheduled for euthanasia. Never before had she felt needed, never known she had something valuable to offer. Her father had never lived with them. She knew him only as a tall, irritable man who owed her mother a lot of money, who used to come by the house once in a while but never lifted her in his arms, who regarded her like a confusing pet. On birthdays she would get a card with a twenty-dollar bill. She'd been nine the last time she saw him. In her sleep one night the dog, for inscrutable canine reasons, clawed at her face, ripping one ear half off, then crawled whimpering under her mother's bed. When she awoke in the hospital, the first thing Miley asked was about the dog, panicked by the thought that no one had fed it. Her mother did not tell her that the dog had been destroyed until after the third surgery. Miley never spoke of it again.

Here is what happened to Armand. Late in Week Four, his daughter Liz, five days into a methamphetamine binge, had a stroke in the bathroom of a West Hollywood nightclub. By the time he got there, she'd been comatose for a night and a day, hooked to a ventilator in a public hospital, a Jane Doe. They'd located Armand through her cell phone. He stayed at her side for over a week, but she did not regain consciousness and never would. The machines would keep her body alive, the doctors said, but Armand would need to make some decisions about whether Liz would have wanted to continue in this way. Something about the word "continue" struck him as unbearable, ghoulish, he told them he could not talk about it, could not really think straight, and he went back to San Miguel to clear his mind and make arrangements to sell his house. One night he drank too much and found himself cruising the boys outside La Parroquia, a habit he'd given up years ago. He met a sweet kid named Wilfredo, treated him to dinner, and took him home. Before dawn Wilfredo opened a window and let two friends in. They beat Armand unconscious and stole several thousand dollars, a Rolex, and his Lexus. Before driving off, they urinated on him. At least they left the wide-screen plasma TV, he would tell himself later, convincing himself this was Wilfredo's doing, a sign of affection or at least pity.

Here is what happened to Richard McMasters. Though his leg would heal, leaving only a puckered scar on his thigh, the antiparasitics would leave him with tremors in both hands that sometimes, when he was excited or anxious, crept into his voice. No matter. His role on the show, and an appearance on *The View*, made him a minor celebrity, and his salon briefly became a hot spot for actresses over forty and L.A.'s most celebrated male strippers. Eventually he sold the business and went to work for E! as a red-carpet correspondent, but it didn't last long; later, he acted in gay porn, though always as a gimp, the butt of a joke. He'd never felt so included as he did on the show, he told his network-paid therapist. In his life he'd never felt so much a part of a family. He knew the others hated him, that they wanted him to lose. Maybe they even wanted him to die. But for six and a half weeks he'd felt, for the first time, that he had brothers and sisters, that his actions meant something to someone other than himself. The world had a place into which he fit just so, he said, a place the exact shape of his body. What good is money without that feeling? That's what everyone's buying, anyway, he said.

Here is what happened to Boby al-Hajj. After four years of mixed success as head of Programming, he was handed the reins of the network's new cable channel, devoted to reruns of classic Reality shows. He bought a vacation home on Catalina Island but rarely went; he spent most weekends in his condo in Silverlake, most nights at his favorite cigar bar. The bartenders, happy to accept his extravagant tips, honored his request that they call him "Bobcat"; the regulars, happy to be treated to the occasional round, held their ridicule until he'd wobbled out the door. He was usually home before midnight, in time to catch the end of SportsCenter and update his profile on Match.com. He had an old nylon-string guitar, on which he would strum Bob Dylan and Beatles songs until he felt he might be able to sleep.

Patel spent years shopping his treatment. Armed with the producer's encouragement, he worked slavishly to perfect the pitch, develop the story lines. He spent months in Jakarta doing research, but he could not get permission to return to the island. He worked every contact he'd ever made. He took meetings, walked on the beach in Malibu with Errol Morris, went to one cocktail party in Bel Air that he left after being twice mistaken for the help. His wife went back to work as a pharmaceutical rep, since they needed health insurance for their youngest child, who was diagnosed with severe autism. The film about the island would never get made. After one exec, pausing at the bottom of the stairs before boarding the studio's jet, said, "I respect the heart of it, Peter, I really do, but the truth is it's just too *dark*," he quit trying.

Alejandra's stepmother, the last connection to her childhood, died of leukemia in Week Six. She had raised Alejandra after her father, a decorated veteran, was killed in a car accident on the New Jersey Turnpike. Her stepmother never let the future math teacher forget how she'd sacrificed for her, how dragging around a child who was not hers had ruined her life. She had a string of boyfriends who drank and smacked her around. Sometimes they smacked Alejandra around. Alejandra left home at seventeen. In accordance with the release she'd signed, she was not told of her stepmother's death until after the finale. The stepmother's last wish was that her stepdaughter, the ungrateful little puta, would lose.

Christopher "Shaneequio" Jones donated most of his winnings to a job-training program for former gang members. He left California, bought a small house in Scottsdale, and succumbed to a desperate love of golf.

Here is what happened to the producer's wife. After a decade of miscarriages, she accepted the fact that she would never have children. She watched this dream float away like a birthday balloon, fading back into the sky until it could no longer be seen. She got back into painting, brought her easels to the terrace and watched the city wake up, watched the fog generate itself each day like a special effect. She painted at dawn, at noon, at dusk, blasting music through the outdoor speakers to forget how quiet the house was behind her. The rooms and hallways filled with canvases, but she never got it right, never quite captured the emptiness she felt breathing up at her from the silent, mechanical city. At a lecture on Abstract Expressionism, she met a tall, reticent man, a high school guidance counselor who was recently divorced, who showed her photographs of his two sons, swelling with a quiet pride that made her knees go soft. He had reddish hair and thick glasses and gave off the air of a chastised boy. He drove to Whittier three nights a week to see his kids, though they usually just sat in a diner or went to a movie. The second time he and the producer's wife met for a drink, he asked if she would like to meet them. She spent the next two months in the grip of a quiet, insistent ecstasy, waiting for the producer to return from whatever unreal, insignificant location he'd gone to this time. A week after she moved in with her new lover, they packed a picnic basket and drove into the Angeles National Forest on a Saturday morning. He had never, he said, made love outdoors, and she realized, as though it had been hidden from her, that she hadn't done so since before her marriage, before the producer showed up at her door. She held her new lover's hand all the way up the freeway, and when they got lost on a service road she could no longer stifle her excitement and she unzipped him while he drove and took him into her mouth. Neither of them saw the tree that had come down in a windstorm the night before. Days later vagrants would strip the wrecked car, careful not to touch the bodies. When they'd gotten everything of value, they set it on fire.

Walter Bernatelli came home to find his brother sacked by depression. The shock treatments had not worked; a progression of ever-more powerful drugs had not worked. He sat at his bedside for days before his brother, whose eyes were crusted shut, hair falling out in clumps, one morning asked if Bernatelli had won the game. Bernatelli said he had. We're rich, he told his brother, and his brother weakly smiled. He sat up and drank some soup, eased out of bed, went to take a bath. Bernatelli sped to the market, spent hundreds of dollars on gourmet food, wine, a bunch of silly balloons. He felt sure things would get better. He's out of the woods, is what Bernatelli repeated to himself. Before he got home, his brother hanged himself.

Gloria Hamm went back to work in the dentist's office. They threw her a small party but never again treated her as a colleague or friend, smiling strangely when she came in, leaving her out of Friday happy hours. A few patients asked her about the show, but most seemed nervous, standoffish, closing their eyes while she silently scaled plaque from their teeth. Most of her winnings went to pay off medical bills. For the rest of her life, she will wake every night wondering if she should have let the surgeons take both breasts.

She should have.

How much more do you want?

How much more do you think you can take?

Our latest market research indicates that demand is endless—and one thing is certain: We've got the supply.

How about Congolese children dying of malaria, for lack of a $1 mosquito net?

How about a home for cripples in Bangladesh, driven to splinters by floodwaters, leaving everyone dead?

Or peasants in Chiapas, whipped for stealing cane, dying of dehydration in the fields? Or aborigines passed out on the streets of Sydney, lifelong alcoholics who never knew their parents? Haitian children orphaned by the earthquake, raped repeatedly in the camps? Bosnian farmers whose fields have been salted? Latvian girls sold to sheikhs in Bahrain?

What do you think of our compelling new lineup? Are these exciting dramas real enough for you?

Too exotic? Too far from home? Just check that box right there. We've got girls in South Chicago, impregnated by HIV-positive uncles. We've got a schizophrenic teenager in Brookline who'll never leave the state hospital. We've got single mothers in what's left of New Orleans, in what's left of South Central, in what's left of Detroit. Iraq War veterans missing limbs and lobes. Grandparents whose children have robbed them blind. Toddlers with tumors—how's that for a title? Psychiatrists who mercilessly beat their wives. We've got girls in Wisconsin, making truck-stop dates with men they've met online; college dropouts with dead dreams and car payments; checkout clerks with type 2 diabetes; men, women, children, who cry themselves to sleep every night.

You name it, we've got it—any misfortune you can dream up.

So many ways to suffer and die, so few slots open in prime time.

You can choose what you want from our fast-growing database. Our new software accepts feedback, allows you to mix-and-match. The search function has been updated. We guarantee you'll find something you like. But if not, please accept our apology. We'll get top people on it before the day's out. Whatever you do, don't change that channel! Reality is an empty canvas, and by god, we will fill it with whatever you need.

But for now, just relax. Don't worry about anything. Why not take a break? We all know you've earned it! Right this way, friend—

we've saved you a seat in first class: real leather, a fluffy pillow, your favorite drink on its way. Kick off your shoes. Take a deep breath. Have you seen our in-flight magazine? We have photos of starlets, interviews with billionaires. We have all the new gadgets, yours at the press of a button. We have four romantic comedies to choose from. We have perfume samples, complimentary champagne, a nice hot towel to wipe the island's grime away.

We're truly sorry for any unpleasantness. We're sorry for any inconvenience or delay. Your pleasure is what matters. We hope you're comfortable now. We hope everything is to your liking. We hope you'll come back.

Would you care for a refill? Can we bring you a blanket?

This is your captain speaking. We're expecting a smooth ride.

The producer never liked to fly. An unavoidable aspect of the job, he stewed about it for days in advance and was often late to airports, costing the network no insignificant amount in overtime. Once on board and buckled into his seat, he would peer down the aisle at the cockpit door; he thought if he could just see through that door, through the front windshield, if he could see what the pilot saw, it would all be less terrifying.

Instead he closes his eyes and repeats a silent mantra, and when the fuselage tilts and gravity reluctantly gives them up he squeezes the armrests and talks to the plane. "Up," he'll whisper. "Get up there. Get up." He never forgets to say it, half believing it's the force of his will that keeps the machine aloft.

But who can say anymore?

After what happened on the island, it seems possible that his will has nothing to do with it. Strangely, he finds this comforting, the lifting of a burden. He orders a scotch, watches the wings waggle, the horizon tilt. He holds the hand of the woman next to him until the island—the unreal island, someone's idea of a terrible, terrible joke—falls away.

What a beautiful day. The sky is clear, the ocean choppy. Sun bathes the cabin, brings a silver drowsiness to everyone on board. The flight attendant's voice is a bubble in warm cream. He leafs through the book in his lap—*Loving God with All Your Mind*— but by the time they've reached cruising altitude, the producer has lurched into thick, dreamless sleep.

The first shudders of turbulence don't wake him. Nor does the pinging of the seatbelt bell. Only when the book slides off his lap, a food cart rolls rattling and smacks into a bulkhead, does he stir; when the overhead compartment dumps two hard camera cases into the aisle, his eyes fly open. He presses his face to the window: the ocean straight down, no sense of altitude or scale. The airplane is banking so steeply that the woman next to him seems to hover just above his shoulder. His ears ache, and outside something streams over the wing—like cloud, or fog, but darker. Somehow, he can't come up with the word.

Screams in the cabin. Passengers clutching armrests.

The noise of the engines grows alarmingly loud. The woman next to him squeezes his hand until it hurts. He studies her face; he can't quite remember who she is, or how she got there, though her loveliness touches him all the same. Her eyes are calm, her mouth forms a word. When he tries to copy it, the sound his own mouth makes is: *Smoke*.

He turns back to the window, to the dark dream blotting out the wing. He says the word again—*smoke*—and then once more. Something about it feels perfect, soothing: as though this were the word he's been trying to say all along.

Stand by, titles.

There's an announcement, inaudible. Flight attendants strap themselves in. The producer does not feel panic. Oxygen masks fall and dance, but he holds her hand and repeats the simple, wondrous word. It's strange how far away the world seems, he thinks, how drastically reduced. It's always like that, when you get right down to it—just a distant ball of struggle and traffic, of overcrowding and pointless argument and endless, unbearable regret, so much less real than we think it is when we're in the middle of it.

Roll titles.

Why not just stay up here, is what he thinks.

Shot of the cockpit: lights flashing, gauges spinning.

Nothing ever happens here, he thinks, and squeezes her hand. Not really.

Dissolve to exterior. The airplane hangs in a motionless sky. Its angle is inscrutable, its aspect ratio completely out of whack.

Thanks, everyone. Great show.

Looks like that's a wrap.

ACKNOWLEDGMENTS

■

The poem excerpted (and mis-excerpted) in Weeks 1 and 4 is "Ulysses," by Alfred, Lord Tennyson. The poem mis-excerpted in Week 3 is "When I Have Fears That I May Cease to Be," by John Keats.

I am grateful to my family for their constant encouragement.

For advice, assistance, and support of one kind or another, I want to thank Vauhini Vara, Stephen Elliott, Scott Hutchins, Eric Puchner, Joshua Furst, Julie Barer, Vidya Vara, Bob Mora, Liz St. John, Dan Rosenheim, Gretchen White, Molly Antopol, and Chanan Tigay. My sincere thanks to the good people of Counterpoint—Jack, Charlie, Adam, Laura, Tiffany, A, and Maren—and my deepest gratitude to Bill Clegg.

© Vauhini Vara

ABOUT THE AUTHOR

Andrew Foster Altschul is the author of the novel *Lady Lazarus*. His short fiction and essays have appeared in *Esquire*, *Ploughshares*, *McSweeney's*, *Fence*, *One Story*, and anthologies including *Best New American Voices* and *O. Henry Prize Stories*. A former Wallace Stegner Fellow and Jones Lecturer at Stanford University, he is currently the director of the Center for Literary Arts at San Jose State University and books editor of *The Rumpus*. He lives in San Francisco. You can visit him at www.andrewfosteraltschul.com.